Pledge

of

Devotion

SherriKayRomig

PublishAmerica
Baltimore

First printing

At the specific preference of the author, PublishAmerica allowed this work to remain exactly as the author intended, verbatim, without editorial input.

ISBN: 1-4137-9119-0
PUBLISHED BY PUBLISHAMERICA, LLLP
www.publishamerica.com
Baltimore

Printed in the United States of America

Pledge

of

Devotion

Dedication

This book is dedicated to my dad, Charles Stickdorn, who always admonished that I could do anything I put my mind to. And to Aunt Ruie, who every time I saw her, encouraged me to keep writing.

Acknowledgments

First and foremost I want to thank my Lord and Savior Jesus Christ for bestowing on me the gift of writing.

I would also like to thank my family for their patience, my husband, Bruce, for his loving support and kind critiquing and my four children Tyler, Taylor, Kierra, and Trent for their help around the house and understanding the words, "…wait a minute I'm writing."

Chapter 1

Elizabeth was standing on the well-worn stool in her parents' bedroom having Mama pin up the hem to her wedding dress. It was just the dress Elizabeth always hoped for. Not too fancy, but just enough extras to make it special.

Ruth was crouched on her knees with pins stuck across the top of her faded, cotton apron front. She couldn't help but smile up at her daughter who looked lovely in the dress. Elizabeth had designed it herself. She had chosen the cream chintz fabric, light weight for her summer wedding. She had wanted lace to overlay the bodice, slightly puffed sleeves with ruffles that met at the elbows. The cream satin sash accented Elizabeth's small waistline. The most difficult part was the scalloped edge at the bottom which was proving tedious to hem. But beyond the loveliness, Ruth had noticed something bothering her daughter for the past few days. It was something she couldn't quite put her finger on. Whenever anything was mentioned to Elizabeth about the wedding preparations she would always put it off for later. True, the wedding wouldn't take place for a couple of months yet, but it didn't seem right for a bride not to be excited to get things done. Didn't she love John, Ruth wondered. Surely she did or she wouldn't have accepted his proposal for marriage. It wasn't like Elizabeth to hold anything back from her. Ruth decided to talk silently to the Lord about it right there on the floor, pins and all. "Lord, you know my daughter is bothered by something, be near to her right now. She needs you, and if she should open up to me give me wisdom, amen." Feeling satisfied Ruth continued with the task at hand.

Elizabeth was antsy just standing on the stool wearing her wedding dress. She felt like one of those mannequins in Bailey's General Store. Shouldn't she be the happiest girl in Pike township? Why did she have this aching gnaw in the pit of her stomach? What would Mama think? Maybe it was just the cold feet that everyone talked about. She found her voice interrupting her thoughts as she spoke aloud.

"Mama?"

"Hmm?" replied Ruth, unable to talk with pins poking out of her mouth.

"Mama," Elizabeth went on nervously. "Did you have cold feet before you married Pa?"

Silently, Ruth whispered a thank you to God for the swift answer to her prayers. "Why do you ask, Elizabeth? Are you having cold feet?"

"I'm not for sure, Mama." Elizabeth bit her bottom lip not sure how she should continue. She could feel the tears starting to come to her eyes. Hopping down off the stool in a careless motion, with hardly any concern for all the pins, she fell to her knees and into her mama's waiting arms. "Oh, Mama," Elizabeth stammered between sobs. "I don't know if I love John enough to marry him. How did you know you loved Pa?"

Ruth allowed Elizabeth a few moments to cry before answering. Speaking comfort to her only daughter, she stroked Elizabeth's long, auburn hair. "There, there now. Is that what's been bothering you?"

Elizabeth, feeling relieved to have let out her feelings, pulled away and began wiping her tears with the back of her hand.

Facing each other as they knelt on the puncheon floor, Ruth reached out to Elizabeth and clasped her daughters hands in hers, speaking gently as they held each others' gaze.

As Elizabeth listened to her mama, she couldn't help but notice the signs of aging on the face before her. The years on the farm and the rearing of four children had certainly taken its toll. But with that winning smile and twinkle in her eyes, Elizabeth still thought mama was the most beautiful woman in the world.

"Elizabeth, I've been worried about you. Is this why you keep putting off making the arrangements for the wedding?" Ruth scolded herself inwardly for not seeing this sooner.

"Sort of, Mama," Elizabeth began slowly. Then the words tumbled out of her mouth like water flowing over rocks in the stream. "I thought being engaged to John would fill that void I seem to have in my heart. But it hasn't. John's a wonderful man. He's considerate and caring, but there are times when I would rather be out riding on Belle across the field than to be with him. Am I wrong for feeling that way?" Elizabeth slowed back down again so mama could soak in the words. "Lately it seems that both of us have been miserable. It wasn't that way with you and Pa was it?"

Getting up from the floor, Ruth sat on the edge of the bed and motioned for Elizabeth to sit beside her. Elizabeth got up with more caution than she plopped down, fearing she would tear out all of her mama's hard work spent on the dress.

"You can't help your feelings, Elizabeth. That's just part of our human nature. But if you felt this way toward John before he asked you, you should have told him how you felt. Marriage is a commitment you make for the rest of your life. You need to chose carefully." Pausing for a moment Ruth continued. "If you truly feel this way then I think there is a young man who you need to tell this to as soon as you can."

"I know, Mama," agreed Elizabeth with a sigh. "It's going to be the hardest thing I've ever done in my life. I do care for John but not enough to marry him. Why do things have to be so complicated? It hurts too much." Elizabeth's stomach started to knot up. "What will John think of me? What will everyone else think?"

Ruth answered assuredly, "Elizabeth, I'm sure you realize that you can't go through life without some hurts and disappointments. That's the way life is. I think deep down inside you already know that. But you shouldn't worry yourself over the thoughts of others. What matters most is doing what is right," Ruth added with affirmation. "And no it's not going to be an easy thing to tell John. But if you would have gotten married and discovered those feelings it would be harder yet. The Lord is faithful to let us know what we need to do if we're faithful and willing to obey. A lot of times that's the hardest part. And since John is human, it's only natural that he will feel some hurt, but I think he will appreciate your honesty." With that said, Ruth changed the tempo in her voice as she continued on. "As for your other question about your Pa and me, well, that's a story in itself."

Elizabeth watched the green color of her mama's eyes brighten as she began to tell of her beginnings with Pa as though it were yesterday. She sat in silence while her mama shared with her everything from how they met, to courting and even when Pa had proposed to her in the chicken coup while she was gathering eggs.

"Yes, I remember your Pa barging right into the hen house that day with a handful of wild flowers," said Ruth chuckling. "He was as nervous as a worm on the end of a hook in the hot summer sun. He told me he had wanted to wait until that evening and ask me in a more proper way, but he couldn't wait that long." Ruth laughed as she talked. "So there I was in the middle of the hen house, a basket of eggs in one hand and a bouquet of flowers in the other. I'm sure that was a sight. But I didn't care. I said yes and we married that fall." Ruth became more serious and spoke with confidence.

"I knew I wanted to be with your Pa for the rest of my life."

Elizabeth got up off the bed and looked longingly out the window. "What am I to do now, Mama? If I'm not to marry John then what?"

Ruth went and stood by her daughter. "I don't have the answer to that, Elizabeth. We will just have to make it a matter of prayer."

Elizabeth turned from the window and gave her mama a hug. "Thank you, Mama."

"You're welcome." Changing the mood Ruth added, "I best get out to the kitchen and get supper ready. Your Pa will be home before you know it." She took off her apron that sported the pins and pulled a fresh one out of the dresser drawer. Before leaving the room, she turned toward Elizabeth. "Here let me help you out of that dress so you can give me a hand in the kitchen."

"All right, Mama." After Elizabeth had gotten out of the dress, she was relieved to put back on her simple tan waist skirt and cream blouse. Mama had already gone into the kitchen and left Elizabeth to carefully tuck the dress away in the chest at the foot of the bed. As she closed the lid, she sighed and prayed in a whisper. "Help me, Lord. I need courage and direction." With that she turned and stepped into the kitchen.

Chapter 2

The kitchen was the largest room in the Grafton home. The wood cooking stove sat near the far outside wall. A large table and chairs graced the middle of the room. Near the back of the kitchen sat a sink with an indoor pump along with a pantry, which held dry goods and canned items. To complete the kitchen, an icebox stood in the corner containing freshly made butter and other things.

Supper was soon ready. Everyone gathered around, and Pa said the blessing. Elizabeth sat in her place at the table. Across from her was Will, her younger brother with that unruly hair of his. He worked at the lumber mill in town, so he wasn't always present for supper. At times he had to make deliveries to the neighboring towns. Elizabeth smiled as she thought about the two vacant seats on each side of the table. Those had belonged to her two older brothers, David and Andrew. David was now a doctor and had a family of his own as well as his own practice. They lived about a six hour ride north on the train. Andrew and his family had the adjoining farm next to Pa's. He and Pa both farmed the land. Most Sunday dinners were shared here with Andrew's family all gathered around the table. She thought of how lively it had been when the boys were still at home. They sure did get into their share of trouble, and Elizabeth remembered growing weary of their relentless teasing.

Elizabeth's smile soon faded and she lost her appetite as she thought of her unpleasant task of speaking to John sometime after supper. No one seemed to notice her pushing her food around on her plate, except Mama.

Ruth took notice of her daughter's silence and uneaten plate of food, but she remained quiet. This was something Elizabeth was going to have to do on her own.

Elizabeth was all too glad to have supper finished. Clearing away the table and helping with dishes helped to keep her busy.

A sudden knock on the door made Elizabeth jump and almost drop the dish she was drying. Seth invited John into the living room to have a seat with him and Will. They made small talk until Elizabeth was finished in the kitchen. Just as she put the last cup away mama came over and squeezed Elizabeth's hand and motioned for her to go. With determination and a stomach full of knots, Elizabeth stepped toward John.

She was glad it was warm enough for them to sit out on the porch this evening. Ohio weather could be so unpredictable. Spring time could be warm one day and frigid the next. She motioned for him to follow her out on the porch where she could say what needed to be said with some privacy.

All was silent except for a few birds in a nearby tree as they both sat down on the creaky porch swing. Then without hesitation they both began to speak.

"John."

"Elizabeth."

That seemed to break the tension of the moment and they smiled and laughed at one another.

John began again, "Go ahead, Elizabeth."

"If you're sure," Elizabeth hesitated.

John gave a reassuring grin and a nod of his head.

Elizabeth could sit no longer. She immediately got up and paced the floor as she talked, keeping her eyes focused on John. "Well, John, this isn't going to be easy for me to say." The nervousness came back to her, but she took a slow deep breath and continued softly. "John, I'm sorry, but I have to break our engagement. I care for you, but I...I'm not sure I love you enough to be your wife. I know I should have said something before now, but I wasn't truly sure. I don't blame you if you're upset with me. You have every right to be. But I've been praying about it and I believe this is what I should do. I'm sorry." Elizabeth's mouth was dry as dust and her palms were sweaty from the wringing she had just given them. She looked away prepared for the worst that was sure to come. There was a moments pause then Elizabeth looked at John. Was that relief she saw in his eyes?

John stood and walked over to Elizabeth as he chose his words carefully. "Elizabeth, I've been doing some praying of my own lately. Actually I was relieved to hear you say what you did. I believe God has called me into the ministry, but I didn't want to say anything to you until I was sure. I knew it wouldn't be fair to expect you to be a minister's wife. I wasn't for sure how I was going to tell you."

"Oh, John, I thought you would never want to speak to me again," expressed Elizabeth with relief. "I'm glad you found God's call on your life. I have no doubt you'll make a fine minister."

They walked back to the swing feeling more at ease and sat down. They swung with a smooth steady motion as the swing creaked out the rhythm.

Elizabeth spoke with concern in her voice. "I feel I need to find my place too. I know I should be content to get married and raise a family, but I feel there is something more."

"I'm sure you'll be the best at whatever you do, Elizabeth. You've always had the determination to do anything you set your mind to. That's one of the things that I admire about you," said John with assurance.

After a while, the coolness of the evening took them inside, where Pa and Will were in a discussion about the progress of the mill. Mama was busy quilting a baby blanket for David and Katherine's little one due in the summer. Everyone stopped what they were doing and looked up as John and Elizabeth stood in the center of the room waiting for their attention.

Elizabeth responded first. "John and I have something to say."

John took over where Elizabeth ended. "Elizabeth and I have decided to break our engagement. It seems that the Lord has other plans for both our lives." He went on to tell about his call into the ministry and that he would be leaving for seminary just as soon as he could get things arranged.

Pa, now standing to his feet reached out and gave John a big, old, bear hug to congratulate him on his new vocation. Will teased about how they would all have to treat him special since he was to be a minister. After Mama gave him a hug and expressed her congratulations, she swiftly gathered everyone into the kitchen, where she served peach pie and coffee to finish the evening.

Late that night when Elizabeth lay in her bed reflecting over the events that had just taken place, she smiled in amazement. She would have never thought things would work out as they did. Sometimes when you didn't know what was going to happen, or wondered why things turned out the way they did Pa always quoted that scripture verse, "All things work together for good to them that love the Lord."

Surely she had seen that tonight. Even though she had an empty feeling inside, and the excitement of marriage preparations were behind her, Elizabeth decided to cling to that verse. She was glad to lay her head down and be at peace.

Chapter 3

Elizabeth awoke to gray skies and rain. She quickly dressed and sat down at her writing desk in front of the window. Her bedroom faced the road. The two other bedrooms across the hall had been occupied by her brothers. She pulled open the top drawer and took out her Bible. She began thumbing through the pages. Usually she would choose a chapter from each of the testaments for her devotions, but she seemed to be drawn in another direction. She remembered something in Matthew about seeking first the kingdom of God. After a little more searching she triumphantly exclaimed aloud, "Matthew 6:33, But seek ye first the kingdom of God, and his righteousness; and all these things shall be added unto you." She read in earnest and went on to read chapter seven where it told to knock and ask.

She closed her eyes right there at her desk and prayed, "Dear God, I'm seeking your will and guidance for my life.

Show me what you want for me. I don't know which direction to turn. Open the doors of opportunity that I might be able to serve you." Elizabeth kept her eyes closed and meditated on what she had just requested of God. A quiet amen escaped her lips, and she opened her eyes once again.

Getting up from her desk she still didn't have any direction for her life, but God had given her peace. She knew that whatever may come her way He would be there.

Will had already gone to the lumber mill when Elizabeth descended the stairs for breakfast, and her Pa had already gone to the barn. She drank a cup of coffee to warm up a bit. The weather was a mite cool and damp this morning.

Ah, she thought. The coffee sure did feel good. She decided to eat a biscuit with some homemade strawberry jam spread on each half.

Mama came to the table and refilled her cup. "Is that all you're going to eat, Elizabeth?"

"I'm just not that hungry, Ma."

"Those brothers of yours were always hungry. It never ceased to amaze me what they did with all that food. They kept it worked off just like your Pa I suppose." Ruth sat down opposite her daughter. "Are you still concerned about last evening?"

Elizabeth looked into her mama's sweet face. Her and Pa always did take their children's hurts to their own hearts. Smiling Elizabeth answered, "I've prayed about it, and I have peace."

"Good, I'm glad," exclaimed Ruth happy to see that Elizabeth gave the situation to the Lord. Changing the subject she added, "Your Pa is going into town this morning. Why don't you go with him? It'll do you good to get out even though it is raining."

"Are you sure you won't need my help with the baking?"

"I'll manage."

"Well, I haven't had a chance to talk with Megan lately.

Maybe I'll have Pa drop me off at their house and pick me up on his way back."

"That sounds just fine," said Ruth glancing out the kitchen window. "It looks like your Pa is about to leave. You best grab your shawl and tell him your plans."

Elizabeth was soon in the carriage beside her Pa. The Hayworths lived about a mile from town. Megan and Elizabeth had gone to school together and remained good friends. They each had obtained their teaching certificates, and Megan was in her first year of teaching at the local school. Elizabeth's heart just wasn't into teaching. She enjoyed the children, but wasn't satisfied in holding a teaching position. She had been more inclined to help her brother David in the medical field. Elizabeth thoroughly enjoyed helping and taking care of others.

Elizabeth and her Pa talked casually on the way. Pa wasn't a real talkative person, but she loved to be with him. He had such insight and wisdom about many things. His personality and character were appreciated by all who knew him.

Except for a few remaining sprinkles, the rain had almost stopped when Pa pulled the team up near the Hayworth house.

"I'll be a couple of hours in town, Elizabeth. I'll pick you up then."

"That's fine, Pa. Thank you for letting me come along with you. I'll be glad to spend some time with Megan. Since Will started courting her, I don't see too much of her except at church."

"Will couldn't have chosen a finer young lady. She has good Christian parents. Your Ma and I have prayed since the day each of you were born that you would all come to know the Lord as you personal Savior. The boys went through that rebellious streak in their teen years, but they all surrendered. We couldn't be happier with all of you." He looked at Elizabeth as he brought the team to a stop and spoke encouragingly. "We haven't stopped praying either. You'll find your place,

Elizabeth, just keep seeking the Lord. He'll never let you down."

Elizabeth was almost disappointed for the ride to end. But once again, her Pa knew exactly what she needed to hear. He helped her down from the carriage, but she didn't let go before she squeezed his hand. "Thank you, Pa, for what you said." "You're welcome, Elizabeth." He then hopped back up into the carriage and started down the road.

Elizabeth hadn't been in the Hayworth house fifteen minutes when they heard a holler coming from the barn. Elizabeth and Megan looked at each other simultaneously and headed off in that direction with Mrs. Hayworth close behind.

When they got inside the barn they found Mr. Hayworth leaning over his oldest son Mark.

Mrs. Hayworth went pale at the sight of her son lying in a listless state. "Is he...?" She couldn't bring herself to finish.

"No, he's still breathing. I think he hit his head when he fell," Jeb Hayworth answered.

"What happened, Pa?" Megan asked with concern.

"Well," began Jeb trying to recollect exactly what took place. "Mark was cleaning out the hayloft when he evidently stepped on a few loose boards, and down he came. I was over there sharpening the plow blade when I heard him holler," he explained as he pointed to where the plow was. "I'll get him into the house and go for the Doc."

"No, wait," Elizabeth interjected instinctively.

All eyes turned on her.

She went on to explain. "You should never move someone without checking to see if they're all right first." She hesitated feeling a bit uneasy for taking charge. She meekly added, "I learned that from my brother David."

Jeb smiled up at her and acknowledged her words and asked for help. Together they were able to rouse Mark to consciousness. He seemed to be all right except for his left leg down near the ankle. It was causing him quite a bit of pain. He said he couldn't move it.

Elizabeth thought he probably broke his ankle although she wasn't a doctor. She told the Hayworths that she would take care of Mark once he was in the house and till the doctor could be reached.

Mr. Hayworth carried Mark inside then went for the doctor. Elizabeth made a splint for his leg so he would keep it still. She wished she had something to give him for the pain. Megan and Elizabeth included Mark in their conversation to try to keep his mind off of his throbbing ankle.

It wasn't long before Jeb was back with Doctor Blevens. Megan and Elizabeth dismissed themselves to the front porch while the doctor took over.

The sun had come out and warmed everything up. Megan and Elizabeth chatted about many things. Megan brought up Will's name often during the course of their conversation. Elizabeth could tell that Megan was very fond of her brother. Elizabeth told Megan of her decision to break off her engagement with John. Being the friend that she was, Megan commended Elizabeth for her courage and committed herself to pray for Elizabeth. That was one of the things that she admired about Megan. She never ridiculed, but listened and gave her the benefit of the doubt.

Doctor Blevens came out the door as Megan was telling Elizabeth about one of her students. Doc Blevens was a big man about six foot. He was broad as an ox and probably just as strong as one too. But he was as gently as a mother cat with her kittens when it came to his patients.

Doctor Blevens turned toward Elizabeth in gratitude and spoke. "Fine job with that ankle, Elizabeth. That's exactly what I would have done in your situation." He winked and continued. "I see you're taking after that brother of yours. David's a fine doctor."

Megan interjected, "How's Mark? Did he break his ankle?"

"As a matter of fact he did, but he's going to be just fine. I set the bone and plastered it with a cast. I told him to stay off of it for several weeks. I also informed your folks, Megan, that I would bring out some crutches in a day or two so Mark can get around on his own."

"Thank you, Doctor Blevens," responded Megan in appreciation.

"Oh, you're quite welcome," he answered happily. "Now if you ladies will excuse me, I need to go out and check on the new Johnson twins."

"Good bye," Megan and Elizabeth spoke in unison.

"Be sure to tell Mrs. Blevens we said hello," added Elizabeth.

"Will do," he replied as he tipped his hat and descended the porch steps.

Shortly after the doctor left, Mr. and Mrs. Hayworth came out to thank Elizabeth for what she had done for Mark. Jeb was sure to tell Seth when he came by to pick up his daughter. He let him know just how much they appreciated Elizabeth's help. Jeb and Eleanor were sure to thank Elizabeth once more before she left.

"So, you were quite the nurse from what I gathered back there," Seth spoke with admiration and a hint of teasing in his voice.

"I just did what David taught me is all. It wasn't much really."

"I'm proud of you, Elizabeth," he spoke in earnest. "You did good."

She smiled up at him and answered, "Thanks, Pa."

Chapter 4

It was near the end of May, and the buds on the trees had matured. The robins had returned from their winter migration. Everything seemed fresh and new. Elizabeth considered it a beautiful day for a walk. As she neared home, she noticed that the windows to their two-story clapboard house had been opened. Even the upstairs windows had been allowed to invite in the spring breeze.

In her hand was a letter from her brother, David addressed to Mama. She hoped everything was all right. She was anxious to hear any news about their family.

In the distance she heard the train whistle, and was once again reminded that it had been three weeks since John had left for seminary. Elizabeth, along with John's parents had been there to see him off. She was happy for John, but it didn't help to calm the restlessness she felt within herself. She still had not found the answer to her questions. What did God want for her? Working three days a week at the post office was not exactly what she had in mind to do for the rest of her life. No, somehow she felt deep inside that she would not remain in New Lexington for the rest of her life. Her heart lurched within her at the thoughts of leaving. She had grown up here. The house, the barn to the left, the chicken coop in the back, and all the land as far as she could see, was the place she called home.

As she neared the back door, home looked even more inviting. The crocuses, hyacinths, and tulips were in full bloom around the house. Elizabeth could tell mama had just hung out the laundry. It flapped in the breeze with a heaviness, like her heart was feeling now. Mama and Papa—how could she ever think of leaving them? She dismissed the thought from her mind as she opened the back door. Mmm… the smell of fresh, baked bread greeted her. Elizabeth savored the fragrance. Mama must have just pulled it from the oven.

"Smells good, Mama," said Elizabeth.

"Thank you, Elizabeth. Why don't you slice yourself a piece while you tell me about your day," returned Mama.

"Uneventful as usual, there's not much to tell. Oh, except for this letter from David," replied Elizabeth as she reached into her skirt pocket to retrieve it, and then handed it to Ruth. Elizabeth spread a spoonful of apple butter on the still warm bread as Ruth opened the letter.

Ruth smiled as she read down through the letter absorbing every detail of news about her family.

Elizabeth was curious and spoke out. "Well, what does he say, Mama? Is everyone all right?"

"Yes, everyone is doing just fine. The girls are growing and Katherine has her hands full taking care of everyone and assisting David in his work." Ruth put the letter down on the table and spoke to her daughter. "Elizabeth, I hope you won't be angry with me, but I wrote to David when you and John broke the engagement. I knew you might want something to occupy your mind, so I wrote and asked David if there was anything that you might be able to do there. That's really what most of the letter is about."

"And?" questioned Elizabeth.

"He says that he could use someone to take Katherine's position. She's been doing light nursing skills to help him out. But with their third child due in a few months and taking care of the girls she's got her hands full. They would all love for you to come and spend some time with them." Ruth finished, not knowing what to expect from her daughter.

Elizabeth sat motionless for a few seconds not knowing what to say. She couldn't believe that just a few moments ago she had entertained thoughts of leaving one day. She never thought it would be so soon. Well, it wouldn't be like she would be leaving for good. She would be back, she was sure.

Ruth interrupted her thoughts. "Is something wrong, Elizabeth? I know I should have talked it over with you first, but I didn't want to get your hopes up in case it didn't work out. You don't have to go, Elizabeth. I just thought…"

"No, no, Mama, it's all right," Elizabeth broke in. "It's just that it took me by surprise is all. Believe it or not I was thinking some of those same thoughts before I came into the house."

"Well, you can take some time to think and pray about it before you decide," cautioned Ruth.

"I'll go, Mama. I have been praying for weeks and things couldn't be any more clear. What about you and Pa? I'll miss you terribly."

"We'll be just fine. It's time you got on with your own life. Besides David and Katherine need you right now," assured Ruth.

Elizabeth went over to the other side of the table where Mama sat and gave her a hug. "Oh, Mama, thank you. I don't know what else to say. I'm excited and a little nervous. I've never really been away from home for such a long period of time."

Releasing her daughters embrace and looking her in the face she saw happiness that had not been there for some time.

"You won't be alone. You'll have your brother, Katherine and the girls. I'm afraid Sarah and Kate are going to get a little spoiled from their Aunt Elizabeth," chuckled Ruth.

"Speaking of my brother," interjected Elizabeth with enthusiasm. "I need to write him back and let him know when to expect me."

"That's all been taken care of, Elizabeth," said Ruth scanning the letter. "David says here he will be expecting you on next Friday's train and enclosed are your tickets."

"Why that's only a week away and there is so much to do, and I want to be sure I say good bye to everyone and..." Elizabeth blurted.

"Slow down, the train's not leaving tonight. You'll have plenty of time. Besides, Sunday you'll be able to say your goodbyes to the church folks. We'll make sure we have Andrew's family over for supper a couple of times before you leave. Saturday evening your brother will get back from his delivery, so you'll have every evening next week to spend some time with him," explained Ruth.

"You make it sound so simple, Mama," Elizabeth returned.

"Well, you just take one day at a time, Elizabeth. I know you're anxious, but everything will work out, you'll see," said Ruth, trying to settle her daughters concerns.

Conversation at the supper table that evening was consumed with talk of Elizabeth's departure. Seth was glad to see his daughter glowing with happiness once again. He was pleased to know she felt a new purpose to her life. He would miss her, that's for sure, but there comes a time for every bird to leave the nest.

Ruth too was happy Elizabeth had chosen to go. This was a big step in her daughter's life but she was sure that God was in it. They loved all of their children, but their only girl would soon be leaving them. She had a feeling that Elizabeth would not return for a long time.

Ruth and Seth, thinking similar thoughts, reached out simultaneously and clasped the other's hand. They exchanged smiles and soaked up the happiness that reflected from their daughter.

Chapter 5

Elizabeth thought it a beautiful day to travel. As she sat in her seat on the train, her eyes scanned the outline of the town before it disappeared from view. New Lexington was a small but growing town. Two main streets intersected in the middle of town. All the places of business surrounded the streets while the farms branched off in different directions.

Alone with her thoughts, she reminisced about the events of the last couple of months. So much had happened. Even though it was she who had broken off the engagement, there was a slight pang of loss in her heart. She still felt certain she had done the right thing. She truly did wish the very best for John but enough of that. She reminded herself of Romans 8:28. "But all things work together for good." *Hmm...* Elizabeth thought as she leaned back onto the seat, *God truly is good.*

The train lulled back and forth in a rhythmic motion as Elizabeth stared out the window. The warmth of the sun shining in the window was enough to put anyone to sleep. But Elizabeth was too excited to sleep. She couldn't wait to get to David's house. Oh, to see the girls whom she hadn't seen since Christmas.

Elizabeth occupied her time until noon with reading a few chapters of a book. Most of the time she spent watching people. They were so interesting. Their mannerisms, actions, and facial expressions were all fascinating to Elizabeth. When the train whistle blew the noon whistle, Elizabeth took out the lunch that her Ma had made for her. She savored each bite as she thought of her parents, not knowing when she would see them again. After eating, she grew tired of sitting and decided to stretch her legs by taking a stroll to the dining car. After purchasing a cup of coffee, she sat down and observed those around her. She watched a father and son engage themselves in a game of checkers. Two ladies sat opposite of Elizabeth dressed quite fashionably. They were talking rather secretively a mile a minute. Elizabeth thought that the two looked like good ones to gossip. Oh, she knew she mustn't judge, so her eyes scanned the dinning car for other passengers to observe. In the far-left corner, Elizabeth's eyes fell on a young couple. They appeared to be newly married. Upon seeing their merriment, Elizabeth decided to finish her coffee and go back to her seat.

When she was settled in her seat, she pulled out her book. She enjoyed reading. If it was a really good book, she found it hard to put down. Opening the book to where a ribbon held her place, she delved back into the story.

Occasionally, Elizabeth looked up from her reading and glanced out the window to view the countryside. Before she had finished the next chapter, she heard the conductor call out, "Next stop Cambridge." But before he could finish, Elizabeth felt herself being thrown to the floor as the sound of grinding metal and shrieking brakes echoed throughout the train followed by a loud, thundering collision. Elizabeth felt her head strike something hard then all went black.

When she became conscious, she heard shouts of frightened passengers, cries of children, and seemingly utter chaos. When her eyes gathered enough energy to open, she was greeted by several people staring down at her. "How do you feel, Miss?" inquired a stranger. "Does anything feel broken?"

"Uh—no," stammered Elizabeth, quite confused at the moment.

"It looks as though you received quite a nasty bump on your head there," continued the stranger.

Feeling quite foolish for lying there on the floor, Elizabeth scurried to get up before anyone could help her. Searing pain sent her hands to cradle her head as she rested on her knees.

"Take it easy there, Miss. It seems as though you may have suffered a concussion," mentioned the stranger kindly.

"I'm all right, really. I just have a headache." Trying to draw attention away from herself she inquired, "What happened?" She slowly rose this time and eased into her seat. As she opened her eyes, her heart fluttered and her cheeks flushed a rosy hue when she realized she was looking straight into the eyes of this stranger who had been watching over her. Dark, chocolate eyes surrounded by a head of thick, dark, hair covered by a Stetson was enough to temporarily forget the throbbing pain inside her head.

The stranger tipped his beige, leather Stetson as he made her acquaintance. "I'm Dirk Hampton, Miss. From what I've gathered, another train misinterpreted the signals and collided with this one. A lack of communication, I've heard. There are several of us from the station who came to help out anyway we could." Feeling concerned for this lady's blow to the head, he asked, "Are you sure you're all right?"

"Um—yes," stammered Elizabeth once again. Oh, why did she seem like a complete fool in front of this stranger? "Is anyone seriously injured?" She questioned before her mind rambled any farther. "I would like to help out in some way."

"Most have suffered cuts and bruises. The most serious were a few with broken bones that have been taken to the nearest doctor. Thankfully, the wreck wasn't any worse," answered Dirk as he stood to his full height of six feet two inches. "I'm sorry I don't believe I caught your name."

"Elizabeth Grafton," spoke Elizabeth with confidence as she tried to stand.

Seeing that she was quite dizzy, Dirk gently put his hands on her small shoulders and helped her back down into her seat. "I know you would like to be of help and that's appreciated, but I think you need to remain seated until your dizziness has passed." Dirk continued before she could protest. "They are sending another engine from Cambridge to bring this train to the station. It should take about an hour or two."

Disgusted with herself for coming across so useless, Elizabeth sank back into her seat and sighed, "I suppose you may be right. I think I'll remain in my seat."

Dirk was glad to hear this young woman wasn't going to put up an argument. He had to admit to himself that she was attractive, especially in that sea green dress that matched her eyes. Her hair was spilling out of her hat that sat crookedly on top of her head, no doubt because of the fall she had encountered. He tipped his hat, "Now, if you'll excuse me, I need to check on the other passengers. It was nice to meet you, Miss Grafton."

"Thank you for your help," came Elizabeth's voice weakly as she looked up into the tanned face once more.

"You're welcome, Miss," replied Dirk as he smiled, revealing the dimples that framed the sides of his mouth.

Elizabeth watched as Dirk made his way to each passenger, doing all he could to make them more comfortable. Was he a doctor she wondered? Where did he come from? Things happened so quickly that she never thought to ask. He must think her rude. But she certainly didn't have any intentions of swooning over every attractive man that came along. One man in her life had caused her enough emotional strain. She didn't need another one.

Just as Mr. Hampton had foretold, at least two hours passed before another engine was sent to pull them to the station. Elizabeth was glad that they were able to get out and stretch their legs in Cambridge before traveling on to Dover. She had seen no more of Dirk Hampton, and for that she was glad. She did not need someone to tell her to sit and rest. She could take care of herself. With a deep sigh, her thoughts turned toward her brother David. She would be so happy to see them again. She was going to enjoy every moment she spent with the girls. And of course she wanted to do her best for her brother in his doctor's office. As the train hummed once more along the tracks, Elizabeth drifted off to sleep.

Chapter 6

As Elizabeth braided the girls' long, blond hair, Sarah quietly played with her doll on the back porch steps. Elizabeth had devoted her full attention to these two precious nieces of hers the past few days since her arrival. David had told her he would need her help in his office starting tomorrow. His doctoring apprentice was going to start tomorrow as well. David had invited him to supper this evening. All Elizabeth knew was that he came from Colorado, but she didn't really care.

"There," Elizabeth announced to Sarah. "I'm finished."

"Oh, goody," replied Sarah hopping down the steps. "Can we swing now?"

"Yes, Sarah, we can swing." It was hard for Elizabeth to deny any request of her nieces.

Elizabeth pushed Sarah in the swing David had made for the girls. It was a long, thick, rope draped over a large branch of the big oak tree, with a slab of smooth wood for the seat. Elizabeth laughed as Sarah giggled with delight and pleaded to go higher and higher. She considered it a mighty feat when she could touch the leaves of the branch that hung out in front of her.

The fun ended all to quickly when Elizabeth announced to Sarah that she needed to go in and help her mama with the supper preparations. Sarah started to protest but was quieted by her aunt's promise to do it again. Hand in hand, they went up the steps and disappeared into the kitchen where Katherine was already busy.

Sarah liked to help her mama, so Katherine put her to work setting the table. Katherine reminded her to set an extra place at the table for their guest. Sarah was filled with questions about this mysterious guest. Katherine informed Sarah that all she needed to know was that it was her pa's new apprentice and he was to be made to feel welcome.

Feeling disappointed, Sarah didn't question any farther but finished her task, talking of how high she had swung in the tree.

The apple pies were just coming out of the oven when Elizabeth heard male voices approaching the house. She had no need to be nervous, but inside her stomach was full of a whole passel of butterflies that seemed to fly in every direction. Determined to not let it get the best of her, she removed the biscuits from the oven, only to drop them at the sound of a familiar voice other than her brother. No, she thought, it couldn't be. It was only her imagination.

"Are you all right, Elizabeth?" asked Katherine who kneeled down to help retrieve the biscuits. She wasn't sure what had come over her sister in law.

"Uh—yes, of course just a little clumsy is all," stumbled Elizabeth for the right words. She had no time to tell Katherine about the familiar voice.

Elizabeth and Katherine arose from the floor just in time as David and his apprentice walked into the room. Elizabeth felt her cheeks flush once again as she was looking into the face of Dirk Hampton. A thousand thoughts flashed through her mind. Him a doctoring apprentice? She couldn't believe it. Elizabeth never thought she would ever see him again.

Having no idea that his sister and Dirk had met, David went on ahead with introductions, smiling with pride at his family. "Everyone, I would like you to meet my apprentice, Dirk Hampton. Dirk, this is my wife Katherine, our two daughters, Sarah and Kate and my sister, Elizabeth."

Dirk nodded his head in acknowledgment and replied, "It's nice to meet all of you." Meeting Elizabeth's gaze he went on. "It's nice to meet up with you again, Miss Grafton. I trust you're feeling better." By her uptight facial expression, he could tell she had not mentioned their meeting to her family.

How dare he ask about her health! Of all the nerve. Was he trying to make her appear incompetent? Elizabeth answered him coolly. "I'm fine thank you, now if you'll excuse me I'll bring in the stew, Katherine." She was glad for any excuse to be out from under the scrutiny of Dirk Hampton.

Dirk hid his smile as Elizabeth turned into the kitchen. He hadn't meant to upset her. She certainly did resemble her brother with that auburn hair and those emerald green eyes. Dirk couldn't help but notice her beauty.

Trying to keep things moving, Katherine motioned for everyone to be seated. "Mr. Hampton, you can sit there beside Kate."

"Thank you, ma'am, and please, call me Dirk," he announced as he smiled at Kate before setting down.

"Very well then, Dirk," returned Katherine as she took her place at the opposite end of the table from her husband. "You may call me Katherine. And please make yourself at home here. We want you to feel like part of the family."

As Katherine was talking, Elizabeth brought in the stew and sat it on the table, then took her place beside Sarah right across from Dirk.

David spoke to Dirk, "I didn't know you had already met my sister."

"Well, sir," Dirk hesitated. "It was during the train collision near Cambridge."

"Oh, yes, Elizabeth did mention the delay. I'm glad there were no serious injuries," mentioned David.

Elizabeth was glad that no one questioned the incident further. She had not told her brother that she had gotten hurt. She didn't want to worry him—besides she was fine. She was glad to hear David ask the blessing so they could get on with the meal. She hoped there would be other subjects to be discussed.

Dirk did not mean to let his mind wonder during David's prayer. He was a complete stranger to this family, and yet he felt this sense of belonging. The only thread that held him to this family was the fact that David's father had led his own father to the Lord. He couldn't help but feel that God had led him in this direction.

After the prayer, Sarah listened to the conversation among the adults like a good little girl, but wanted to be a part. So, without hesitation she questioned Dirk. "Mr. Dirk, are you going to marry my Aunt Elizabeth?"

Elizabeth felt that she surely had never been more embarrassed in her life. And she wasn't about to look Dirk Hampton in the face. David and Katherine tried to stifle their laughter.

Before anyone could say a word, Sarah answered her own question without missing a beat. "I guess I forgot you have to ask papa's permission to court her first."

"Out of the mouths of babes," chuckled David.

Dirk took it all in stride and smiled so broadly that both of his dimples shown through his tanned face. He stole a glimpse at Elizabeth, who was flushed a deep crimson from the top of her head to the bottom of her delicate chin then replied. "I'm afraid I can't marry your aunt, Sarah. You see

I've just met her. You need to get to know someone before you just up and marry them."

That was all the explanation the young girl needed. "Oh, okay," and with that she went on to finish her dinner.

The rest of the evening went rather smoothly with conversation revolving around Dirk and how things were in Colorado. Elizabeth was glad to be finished so she could excuse herself into the kitchen, taking Kate along with her. Elizabeth knew it was rude of her, but she hoped that Dirk would not linger too long after dinner. She thought the more distance she kept from him, the better it would be.

Soon after the dessert of apple pie, Dirk rose from his seat and spoke with gratitude. "Thank all of you for the fine evening, but I best be getting back to the boarding house. Mrs. Flanagan locks the doors at nine o'clock sharp."

"I'll walk you out, Dirk," said David standing to join him. "I'll fill you in on what we will be doing tomorrow."

"Sounds good," replied Dirk taking his Stetson from the hook beside the door and placing it on his head. Before leaving he turned around one last time to speak. "Thanks again Mrs. — uh excuse me, Katherine, for the fine meal. The apple pie was delicious."

"You're quite welcome, Dirk," answered Katherine smiling. "But I can't take all of the credit. Elizabeth made the apple pies."

Oh, why did Katherine have to say anything, thought, Elizabeth.

"Well, then, Elizabeth," complimented Dirk as he tipped his hat and focused his attention on Elizabeth. "My thanks to you for the delicious pie."

Feeling completely uneasy, Elizabeth looked up only long enough to answer in a monotone voice, "You're welcome." She quickly turned her attention to young Kate who was playing on the floor.

Not wanting to be left out, Sarah piped up and pleaded.

"Please come back, Mr. Dirk. I want to show you how high I can swing."

"Well, now, with an offer like that, how can I refuse?" winked Dirk to Sarah who was beaming with pride. He was pleased Sarah had taken to him. He stole a glance Elizabeth's way, but she was too intent at her play with Kate.

But Kate didn't want to be outdone by her sister and called out, "Night, Mr. Dirk."

"Good night, little Miss Kate. Sweet dreams." Dirk turned around and he and David were gone.

Chapter 7

Elizabeth was only too glad to be busy in David's office. There was so much to learn. She was mainly supposed to help David keep up with his medical supply list. He had told her that he would teach her what medications were for what symptoms and treatments. He also wanted her to learn the various instruments he used in case he needed assistance in surgery. At the moment, Elizabeth was going through his files familiarizing herself with his patients.

All of the sudden she heard commotion coming from the back door. She got up from where she sat at David's desk to check when Dirk and David came carrying a man who appeared to be wounded. It looked like Dan Turner, a widower who lived on the outskirts of town.

"What happened?" she questioned concerned for the man who was lying there semi-conscious and bleeding.

David turned and answered her straightforward. "He was

shot, a hunting accident." David didn't have time for lengthy explanations. This man's life was in his hands.

"Is there anything I can do?" asked Elizabeth as she watched them remove the blood soaked shirt.

"Yes," came David's curt answer. "You can get the carbolic acid over there so Dirk and I can sanitize our hands."

Elizabeth did as she was told. She swabbed the carbolic acid onto each of their hands. Dirk whispered a thank you, which made Elizabeth flustered. But in no time, he was serious for the task which lay before him.

David was assisting Dirk this time instead of the other way around. David wanted to give Dirk as much hands on training as he could to prepare him for when he would be on his own.

Elizabeth couldn't help but to look on as Dirk worked to save Dan's life. His hands worked quickly and steadily. Her mind went back to their meeting on the train, and the way he went about caring for others. She couldn't help but admire that quality.

It was a tedious operation, trying to remove a bullet, and Elizabeth figured they would both be needing some coffee later. There was a small stove mainly used for heating the office, but Elizabeth set out to make the men some coffee.

Feeling guilty for accomplishing next to nothing the past hour, Elizabeth went back to work on filing David's patients in alphabetical order. By the low murmur of their voices and the gathering of instruments, Elizabeth guessed them to be nearly finished. It was late in the afternoon. She thought if they didn't need her help she would leave for the day. But no sooner had the thought entered her mind when she heard a loud wrapping on the front door.

Mr. Harrison came inside nervous and out of breath. "Where's the Doc?"

Before Elizabeth had a chance to answer, David came from the back room. "What is it, Jack?"

"It's Carl Olsen over at the mill. He was cutting some

boards, and he pushed one through too far and the saw nearly took off his hand."

Without hesitation David asked, "Where's Carl now?"

"He's still at the mill."

David went into the back room and returned quickly. "Jack, take this cloth and wrap it around Carl's hand to help stop the bleeding. Get him over here as soon as you can while I ready a place for him here."

Jack Harrison was soon on his way, while David sent Elizabeth to the house for extra pillows, towels, and blankets.

Meanwhile, Dirk finished up with Dan Turner who was resting comfortably. Dirk had been able to remove the bullet and sew him up without complications.

By the time Elizabeth came back, David had transferred Dan to a makeshift cot in the back corner. Jack had brought Carl in and left him in the care of David and Dirk. Jack had said that he would ride out to the Olsen place and give Carl's wife the news.

Elizabeth had brought Dirk and her brother something back from the house to eat. Right now they were too occupied with Carl to think about food. Dirk was assisting David this time.

With the stove and all the people gathered in one place, it soon became quite warm. Elizabeth found herself with a cloth dabbing the perspiration from off the forehead of her brother and Dirk. David kept busily working on Carl's hand as if she hadn't even touched him. Dirk on the other hand always looked up and mouthed the words thank you, making her keenly aware that he seemed to enjoy the attention.

She watched the tension in her brother's face as he carefully stitched the hand back together. Elizabeth had to admit that David stitched very well. It would heal nicely. The only words that were expressed during this time was David explaining the procedure to Dirk as he went along.

When the surgery was complete, David breathed a deep

sigh and removed his soiled, medical coat, which was splotched with blood.

Dirk removed his coat as well and asked with concern, "Do you think he'll loose the hand?"

David tried to sound optimistic as he replied. "He's lost a lot of blood, but everything went well. He's not carrying a fever so that's a good sign. So many tendons and nerves were severed though I'm afraid he won't gain back the full use of it."

"That's sort of what I figured."

"I would like to keep the men here overnight," David stated.

Before David could say anything more, Dirk cut in, "I'll stay. You go be with your family."

"Are you sure? It won't be too comfortable sleeping in a chair."

"I'll be fine. Besides, there's an extra pillow and that's about all I need right now."

"Thanks, Dirk, I'll be in first thing in the morning."

David and Elizabeth were about to head out the door when she remembered the stew and biscuits she had brought earlier in the day. Elizabeth figured Dirk would be hungry before morning, so she decided to leave it there. Turning around she met his gaze and quietly stated, "If you get hungry there's some stew and biscuits near the stove."

To her surprise Dirk thanked her curtly and turned and walked away. He didn't seem the type to lack for words. Dirk's silence puzzled her. He must be very tired or deeply concerned about the two men who lay in the back room, she thought. Stepping outside she scolded herself for letting herself become interested in his well being. To satisfy herself she changed her attitude and decided that she could care less if he ate or not.

She and David spoke very little on the way home. Elizabeth could see the tiredness in his eyes and the exhaustion in his posture as he drove the wagon.

Being the first one to enter the door, Elizabeth was bombarded with cheerful chatter from the girls. When David entered, after unhitching the team the girls ran and practically jumped into his arms. Despite being tired, he smiled and enthusiastically took turns picking up the girls high into the air while spinning around. He was never disappointed as their squeals of delight rang throughout the house.

Katherine had kept supper warm for them. The warm food and the cheery home put Elizabeth in much better spirits than when she left the office.

Sarah and Kate were both eager to tell of the activities of the day. Sarah went first telling of Mrs. Shank's visit. Sarah was sure to express her frustration at Arthur Shanks, the oldest boy in their family. He was two years older than Sarah was. Apparently Arthur had yanked on Sarah's pigtail and criticized her lack of ability at trying to catch him. Before Kate had a chance to speak, Sarah went on about Abigail Shanks who was the same age as herself. Elizabeth listened with a hidden smile as Sarah explained Abigail as being a show off. Sarah went on to say that the whole time they were visiting Abigail did nothing but brag on herself. No, matter what was said she could do better.

"I was glad when they left, Pa."

"Now Sarah," David spoke in a tender manner toward his growing daughter. "We may not agree with a person's actions or attitudes, but we are to treat them kindly when they are our guests. Do you understand?"

"Yes, Pa," Sarah answered in a deflated tone.

Leaning over and placing a kiss on her forehead David concluded, "That's my girl."

Katherine cleared her throat to get the attention of her husband, and nodded in Kate's direction.

Kate, feeling left out of the conversation, looked forlorn with her arms crossed in front, and a long face about ready to cry.

David smiled and picked her up and sat her on his lap and asked, "And how did Kate's day go?"

Kate's mood quickly changed at the attention of her Pa. And with much excitement, she told of how she got pecked by the rooster when she was in the coop with Ma. She also shared with delight the news about the new kittens in the barn. Oh, if there was some way to capture the moment before her Elizabeth thought. She looked at the affection that was taking place between David and his daughters. To see them look up to him with admiration, and to hear them express everything that they hold inside. Family was so precious Elizabeth thought. She hoped to have one some day of her own.

Chapter 8

Dirk had been in and out of the office all day since David had dismissed Dan and Carl. He had hoped to catch up to Elizabeth to give her a proper thank you for the food last evening. His mind had been so tired, he hadn't cared whether he ate or not. Each time he came into the office he had just missed her. Dirk was disappointed when David told him he had given her the rest of the day off. That meant that he would not see her again until Sunday at church. Even then he wasn't sure if he would get the chance to just talk to her. It appeared that she endlessly tried to avoid him. She always seemed to be on pins and needles when she was around him. *Maybe there was someone else* he thought for a moment. *No, there mustn't be or Sarah would have informed me for certain.* He just couldn't figure out Elizabeth. He couldn't believe that she would still be upset about their meeting on the train. He had meant no harm by wanting to help her. The rest of the patients wouldn't see him at all if he didn't get busy, so he must stop thinking about who he couldn't help.

Elizabeth was enjoying her time off. She stopped by the general store to purchase a few items before going home. Dover was certainly larger than New Lexington. So many streets and places of business. From David's office on Factory Street, she had to make a right onto Third Street. The general store sat on the corner of Third and Market. It bordered the town square. How much different this was from home. At the thought of home, her mind raced to her folks. She hoped they were doing well. She longed to have an afternoon visit with Megan and tell her about things here. Elizabeth wondered if Megan would teach at the school this coming school year. The Carson twins were another year older and know doubt would be more mischievous. Megan would certainly have her hands full.

Before Elizabeth got inside the house, she could hear Sarah singing. She couldn't recognize the words, but the melody sounded familiar. Sarah often sang the tune to a hymn sung in church and inserted her own words. Elizabeth opened the door to find Sarah and Kate playing church. Elizabeth couldn't help but chuckle. Sarah, Kate and their dolls made up the small congregation of four. Elizabeth sneaked in quietly so she wouldn't disturb their play. Upon hearing Sarah's boisterous singing, Elizabeth's assumption that Sarah was the song leader was confirmed. Elizabeth was curious as to who would be the minister. But before she could wonder any further, the girls looked up in unison to find their Aunt Elizabeth standing by the door.

"Oh, Aunt Elizabeth, come play with us. Will you pretend to be the minister? Please!" pleaded Sarah with delight.

Before Elizabeth could reply, Katherine came into the room with a smile on her face and inquired, "Who wants to help me make cookies?"

"Me," chorused both of the girls getting up from the floor to surround their Ma in excitement.

"Okay," Katherine acknowledged. "But first you must wash your hands."

Without having to be told twice, Kate and Sarah were gone. Elizabeth smiled at Katherine who was still standing in the room. "Thank you, Katherine, I'm not sure how fine of a sermon I would have given."

Katherine laughed and replied teasingly, "I would like to sit in on the next service to hear you."

They both gave out a chuckle as they entered the kitchen.

Elizabeth did more observing than baking as she watched the delight on the girls faces as they helped their Ma. Even though Katherine could have gotten the cookies done more quickly without their help, she seemed to take pride in teaching her girls.

After the cookies were baked, the girls went outside to play while Katherine and Elizabeth cleaned up the kitchen.

"So, Elizabeth," chimed Katherine as she began to wash up the dishes. "What do you think of Dirk Hampton?"

Elizabeth could feel her face flush slightly and she shot Katherine a look of contempt. She was not certain of how to respond, so she spoke curtly, "He's nice, I suppose."

Katherine stopped washing long enough to chuckle softly before speaking. "Oh, come now, Elizabeth. Is that all you can say about a man who makes you tongue-tied?"

"Katherine," began Elizabeth, feeling herself becoming frenzied at the mention of his name once again. "I can't believe you would make such a remark. I did not come here to find a husband, if you'll remember. I came here for a change."

Katherine was quite taken back by Elizabeth's rebuttal. She hadn't known Elizabeth would respond so defensively. "I'm sorry, Elizabeth, I didn't mean to upset you. I was only teasing you since all the other young ladies in town would love to be in your shoes. I truly meant no harm." Katherine spoke in a concerned, apologetic tone. She had never seen Elizabeth get so upset. She hesitated before going on. "Is there something bothering you, Elizabeth, something that you would like to talk about?"

Elizabeth turned to face Katherine with a softened countenance and a repentant heart. "I'm the one who should be sorry, Katherine. I never should have spoken to you that way. But you're right you know. Dirk Hampton does make me tongue-tied and I don't like it one bit. I don't want it to bother me like that."

Katherine moved over to the table and pulled out two chairs. She motioned for Elizabeth to join her before she spoke. Katherine tried to choose her words carefully before she mentioned them aloud. "Elizabeth, what you're feeling is a natural response to an attractive young gentleman who happens to give you attention."

"But I don't want the attention. I'm not ready for another relationship," Elizabeth sighed with exasperation.

"Well, I don't necessarily mean a courtship. I just think Dirk needs a friend. He hasn't been here that long, and his apprenticeship with David doesn't leave him much time socially. I think that's why he finds your company so enjoyable. You're both about the same age and share some common interests. Just give him some time to get to know the others in town. A few of the young men do speak to him after services on Sunday. And I know there are several young ladies at church who would love to be in your place. I guess what I'm trying to say is, for right now just be his friend."

Feeling somewhat better about the situation, Elizabeth smiled slightly and nodded her head in agreement. "I guess you're right. Thank you for listening and understanding. I'll try to remember what you said about being a friend."

"Good, I'm sure things will work out fine. And remember, Elizabeth, anytime you need to talk I'm here."

"Thank you," spoke Elizabeth sincerely.

"Now," said Katherine getting up from the table. "I'm going to check on the girls, they've been outside for quite awhile."

That evening after supper and family devotions, Elizabeth went outside to take a walk before going to bed. She inhaled a deep breath of summer air. A breeze stirring the trees indicated that sleep would be more comfortable tonight. It was a beautiful evening. Elizabeth looked up to see a sky arrayed with thousands of twinkling stars. Only a sliver of the moon could be seen, it seemed to be sitting crookedly in the night sky. The rest was hidden in the ebony shadows of the darkness. She smiled to herself at the thought of God looking down upon His creation and being pleased. Elizabeth listened to the night sounds. The only sounds she could hear was the croaking of the frogs in conversation and an occasional call of a whippoorwill from a nearby tree. Truly, she thought, God is good. Elizabeth contemplated her blessings as she walked the fence line that ran parallel with the road. She had so many things for which to be thankful. Then her thoughts turned toward Dirk. He had no family here and not many friends of yet. She began to feel guilty for shutting him out. It wouldn't be easy, but she would try her best to be a little more friendly. She decided to think of him like a brother, that way she would feel more herself and not get so tongue-tied.

Even though she was struggling with Dirk's friendship, peace remained in her heart. Surely God had placed her here.

Chapter 9

Elizabeth was in David's office taking inventory for his monthly order. She knew he didn't like to get too low on medicines and supplies. There wasn't very much storage space in his two-room office next to the general store. The front part of David's office contained a small, oak desk and a large cabinet that held medicines which were kept under lock and key. Another smaller cabinet sat along the opposite wall. It held other supplies such as cotton swabs, tongue depressants and bandages. The back room was used for examinations and operations if necessary.

It was hard for Elizabeth to believe it was the middle of the summer. Where had the time gone? She had kept busy doing everything from changing bandages to assisting in the delivery of several babies. She was glad that she hadn't had to spend much time with Dirk, besides those times she had to assist him in setting a few broken bones. Her idea of thinking of him like one of her brothers had helped. He took his apprenticeship seriously. She did have to commend him though; he was so gentle with every patient from the aged to the young. He took the time to listen and attend each one with patience. He would make a good doctor, she was sure.

Well, she thought, disgusted with herself, meditating on Dirk Hampton wasn't getting her inventory done. So back to work she went, sitting on a low, three legged stool hovering over the supplies in the cabinet. "One, two, two bottles of carbolic acid," she voiced aloud. She wrote her findings on paper and continued on. Very shortly she announced as if there were someone listening, "I am finished."

Just as she was standing up, Dirk came from the back room. His nose was buried in a medical book, stuffed full of scribbled notes on many pages. Not watching where he was going, Dirk collided into Elizabeth, sending her forward into a heap on the floor. His book had popped out of his hands, sending its pages flying and scattering his many notes abroad.

Dirk had no idea Elizabeth was even there. He was quite sorry he had not been paying more attention to where he was going. *Surely,* he thought, *she will not understand. It will just give her another excuse to keep her distance. I may as well apologize and get it over with, for her wrath is sure to come.* But quite the contrary occurred. She took him totally by surprise. Just as he was about to seek her forgiveness, he heard a bubbling chuckle escape her lips. Then she broke out into jovial laughter, the first he had heard from her. It was a refreshing sound. He couldn't help but notice her beauty. He reached down to help her up, apologizing through his own laughter. She accepted, and let him clasp both of his hands around hers, pulling her up to stand.

Now feeling foolish, Elizabeth stepped back and brought her hands up to cover her mouth. "I'm sorry, I shouldn't be laughing at you," she apologized with twinkling eyes. "It just happened so fast. The look of surprise on your face was quite a sight." Elizabeth blurted out with more laughter then stifled it and composed herself. "I'm truly sorry, honest."

Dirk brought his laughter to a halt as well. "I'm to blame. I should have been watching where I was going." He didn't know exactly what to do, so he flashed Elizabeth one of his biggest smiles and decided to take advantage of the moment and asked, "Can we put the past aside and be friends now?"

Taken back by this dashing young man, Elizabeth felt guilty about how coldly she had treated him and decided that it wouldn't hurt to be friends. "Yes," she spoke softly. "I've been rude and self centered. I never should have acted the way I have toward you," she concluded in a serious tone.

"Then why? Was it something I did or said?" questioned Dirk, his tone sobering.

"No, it's nothing you've done. It's something I'd rather not talk about right now." spoke Elizabeth avoiding his eyes. She changed the subject abruptly. "It looks like David's office could use a straightening up." And she began to pick up the inventory sheets.

Dirk said no more. He knew his limits. He joined in her efforts by picking up his book and his note-filled papers, shoving them securely into the medical book.

They worked on in silence until they both rose to their feet. Elizabeth broke the stillness. "Well, I need to be on my way and see that this order gets to the post office." She carefully folded and placed the order in an envelope as she spoke.

Before she was able to get out the door, Dirk asked, "Would you mind if I walked with you? The boarding house is just past the post office."

Elizabeth bit her lower lip hesitatingly, "I suppose there would be no harm in that." And she turned on her heels, leaving Dirk to lock up the office. She hoped to gain a good head start. *At least it wouldn't be a far walk. After all, he did have to go to the boarding house and the post office was on the way,* she reasoned with herself.

It didn't take long for Dirk to catch up with her. The conversation was light. They talked of their work mostly and the patients they had assisted.

As they neared the post office, Elizabeth thought she heard someone call her name. She found that strange because very few people in town addressed her by her first name. She stopped and turned around.

"Is something wrong, Elizabeth?" Dirk asked with wonder.

"No, I don't think so, I just thought I heard someone call my name. It's silly, I know. How can I hear anything with all the hustle and bustle of the town. I guess maybe it's just my imagination." She turned back around and continued walking.

The voice came again, this time louder. "Elizabeth!"

Dirk heard it this time and turned around as well. "Look, over there," motioned Dirk across the street. "There's a man waving. He seems to think he knows you."

"Where?" questioned Elizabeth as she turned to find the voice.

"Right over there," pointed Dirk. "Across the street by the livery."

"John?" spoke Elizabeth weakly. *What was he doing here?* she thought.

"John who? Do you know him?" inquired Dirk, as he watched the color slowly drain from Elizabeth's face.

John dodged carriages and people until he made it safely across the wooden boardwalk and stood facing Elizabeth. "Hello, Elizabeth, how are you?"

She stammered to find the words. "I'm fine thank you." Her mind was whirling in a hundred different directions. "What a surprise. I thought you were in seminary."

"Oh, I am," assured John. "I'm off for a few weeks on break between semesters. We're on our way to see my folks." John said, as happy as he could be.

"We?" asked Elizabeth, not sure she wanted to hear the answer.

"I'm sorry," John apologized. "I thought you already knew. I got married a couple weeks ago."

"Married?" Elizabeth asked as she felt her legs turn to melting butter. She knew she had no right to feel upset, and she certainly didn't want her feelings to show. After all, their break up had been a mutual agreement. But she didn't understand how he could get married in such a short time. She never dreamed she would meet him again under such circumstances. She was completely shocked.

Dirk noticed that Elizabeth was trembling and unsteady on her feet. Hoping he wasn't out of place, he placed his hands at her bent elbows to support her. He didn't know what the relationship between the two was or had been, but whatever was going on, Elizabeth was not amused.

John interrupted Dirk's thoughts by answering Elizabeth. "Yes, I met Melissa in the little church I've been attending. We just had a small family wedding in her parent's home, and since I have some time off, I wanted to take her back home and show her the farm."

"Oh, I see," Elizabeth spoke calmly, regaining her composure. "Congratulations, John, I'm happy for you." Elizabeth suddenly realized Dirk had been standing there the whole time, and she hadn't introduced the two. What would she say? She hesitated, then stepped sideways to face both John and Dirk. "John, I would like you to meet Dirk Hampton. He's David's apprentice. And Dirk, this is John a friend of our family." *There*, she thought, *that's all Dirk needs to know.*

Dirk and John exchanged handshakes and friendly greetings.

"Well," broke in John. "I'd best get back to Melissa; I left her at the motel to freshen up. We thought we would spend the night here and go to church in the morning. I was hoping I would get the chance to talk to David while we're in town."

Elizabeth knew her brother would be happy to see John, but she wasn't about to be the one to invite him over to the house. "David's making some routine calls on a few of his patients right now. I don't know when he'll get home, but I'll let him know you're in town."

"Thank you, Elizabeth," John said. He stepped back off the boardwalk and continued. "Sorry, I've got to be on my way. It was good to see you again, Elizabeth. Nice to meet you, Dirk." He turned and headed back toward the motel.

Elizabeth's drained emotions caused her to feel nauseated. She thought for a moment she might collapse, but there was nothing to hold on to. She didn't want to make a spectacle of herself right there in town.

Dirk came to her rescue once again by taking her hand in his and steadying her. "Elizabeth, are you all right? You look a little pale."

"Uh-yes, yes I'm fine, really," she declared uneasily. "It was just a surprise to see him, that's all." She took a deep breath, determined not to appear weak in front of Dirk as she had before. She suddenly realized Dirk had a hold of her hand. How dare he assume she needed his help! Pulling away from him she announced curtly, "If you'll excuse me I need to be getting home to help Katherine with the dinner."

"But Elizabeth," Dirk questioned. "What about the post office?"

"Post office?" Elizabeth had completely forgotten her task. She looked down at the envelope that contained the inventory order. She had entirely crumpled one side during her conversation with John. Pressing it against her skirt to straighten it out, she replied, "I think I'll just wait and mail it first thing Monday morning. I really need to get going." She turned and scurried away down the boardwalk in the opposite direction.

"Beth," Dirk called after her. But it was no use. Dirk sauntered away in the direction of the boarding house. It was going to be hard to study on medical terms tonight. His thoughts were already consumed with Elizabeth. He hadn't meant to get so close to her; he just reacted automatically when she wavered. His heart pounded inside his chest at the thought of her beauty and the sweet lilac scent of her hair. His occupied thoughts turned to John. Who was he? How much of a friend was he? Dirk had a lot of unanswered questions, but one thing he did know was that this "friend" had ruined a perfectly good day.

Elizabeth finally slowed down her pace when she reached the end of town. What had Dirk called her, "Beth?" Her Pa had been the only one to call her that, and only when she was younger. *Does Dirk think I'm too young to take care of myself? I don't need his help. Why did I consent to that walk to the post office? I would not have met up with John.* Her heart began to beat in furry and she unconsciously increased her pace. *Why did John have to seek me out? Was it just to throw up his marriage in my face, to get back at me for breaking our engagement?* She abruptly came to a halt and sighed. She reasoned with herself. *No, John would never do that, he's not that way. What am I thinking?*

With her mind full and her heart heavy, Elizabeth neared the house not the least bit hungry. *After dinner dishes are washed and put away,* thought Elizabeth, *I think I'll take a walk down to the creek. I need to sort out some things and pray, pray indeed.*

Chapter 10

Normally Elizabeth immensely enjoyed Sunday; the day set-aside for going to church. Elizabeth had received much help from Pastor Thompson's sermons, and the fellowship of the congregation was stimulating. Having a day to herself was an added bonus. But the smile quickly faded from her lips as she harbored some negative thoughts about today. Even though the sun was shining on the outside, it was cloudy in her heart. She dressed deliberately slow trying to take up time. She didn't know exactly why. Church would start on time whether she was ready or not. Elizabeth was in and out of three dresses before she decided on the creme waist skirt and ruffled blouse. She didn't know why she was so concerned about what John would think. What should it matter what she wears? Was she jealous, she questioned herself? No, she argued within. She was truly happy for him, she reassured herself. Yesterday had just been quite a shock. She hadn't expected to see him so soon, especially not married. Trying to dismiss John from her mind, she pinned up her hair, chose a matching bonnet, and descended the stairs.

It seemed as though David could sense his sister's nervousness. He drove the team at a leisurely pace as he pondered about the question he was about to ask her. He hesitated, then proceeded. "Elizabeth, would you mind if we invited John and Melissa over for dinner after church?"

Elizabeth felt sure her heart skipped a beat. She thought being in the same church service would be bad enough, but dinner as well? The whole afternoon in their presence? But how could she say no, it was not her home. David could invite whomever he wanted, although she was grateful that he had considered her feelings. She knew she would have to get over her feelings sooner or later; it may as well be today. She looked up at her brother and meekly spoke, "That would be fine, David."

Katherine, who had taken it all in, turned to Elizabeth and asked with concern, "Are you sure? We don't want to make you uncomfortable."

"No, I'll be fine really," Elizabeth replied with more assurance.

Katherine smiled and nodded, "If you're sure."

Elizabeth returned the nod and prayed silently for the Lord to help her through. She knew she shouldn't let it bother her so. Maybe if she devoted her time to the girls, the day wouldn't be so bad. *One thing's for sure*, she thought, *I won't have to occupy the same pew. Dirk always sits on the end near David, and I usually sit on the opposite end beside one of the girls.*

Elizabeth was disappointed when the service ended. It had been hard for her to put her heart into the singing. She felt bad that she couldn't remember anything Pastor Thompson spoke about. She glanced up as she was stepping out of the pew. There was John and his wife near the back. They must have gotten there late.

So, that was Melissa. She was shorter than Elizabeth and had light brown hair which complimented her cornflower blue eyes. She was dressed in a lavender dress with a matching bonnet. *They make a nice couple,* thought Elizabeth. She was glad she had no jealousy in her heart.

Elizabeth lingered in the aisle way a few moments talking to a couple of young ladies near her age. Not too far away was Dirk being thronged with young ladies as well as a few young men. Everyone seemed to enjoy Dirk's company. It didn't even bother her when he looked her way smiling. She returned the smile and gave a slight wave of her hand. She dismissed herself from her company's presence and made her way outside. She didn't want to keep David waiting.

After they arrived at home, Katherine and Elizabeth set about making dinner preparations. When John and Melissa arrived, Melissa offered to help, but Katherine wouldn't hear of such a thing.

Dinner went smoothly enough. The chicken and noodles tasted heavenly with the fresh green beans. The raspberry pie complimented the meal. Sarah was the only one who elected to go without pie. She doesn't like the seeds.

With the dishes cleaned and put away, Elizabeth graciously excused herself for a ramble in the woods with the girls. Despite the humid temperatures, it was a beautiful, sun filled day. There wasn't a cloud in the resplendent, azure sky. Because the woods was so densely populated with trees of various kinds, Elizabeth thought it seemed to be a little cooler.

Kate and Sarah walked ahead of their aunt, picking the trillium that grew in abundance. Sarah spotted and leaped after a butterfly, trying to catch the specimen. Kate followed in pursuit of her sister. As the butterfly flew to greater heights, the girls lost interest and came back to retrieve their flowers.

A little further, they came across a dead tree that was laying in their path. Kate and Sarah stepped up on one side and down the other. In the other hand, Elizabeth hadn't walked the length of a fallen tree in years. She shared with the girls a game she played when she was about their age. She explained how that she pretended the fallen tree was across a high ravine. She would be the only one to cross and rescue a helpless person in danger. Oh, she thought as she stepped up on the old, hickory tree, *what an imagination I used to have when I was younger.* The girls were excited at the very idea of their aunt's adventures.

"Walk across the ravine, Aunt Elizabeth," suggested Sarah full of enthusiasm for this new game.

"I don't think so, Sarah," refrained Elizabeth. "That was just something I pretended to do a long time ago."

"Please," pleaded both Sarah and Kate.

"Now, you really have someone to rescue. Me and Kate will go down to the other end of the tree and pretend we're in danger."

Elizabeth gave out a chuckle as she thought of playing out one of her adventures of long ago. Seeing that they wouldn't have it any other way, she consented. "All right," she stated as she stepped onto the broad trunk. "But only one time."

"Goody!" exclaimed the girls jumping up and down in their excitement. They ran down to the other end as promised and waited for their aunt to rescue them from danger.

With her arms extended out on both sides for balance, Elizabeth began her journey. Most places were no trouble, but there were several slippery mossy places along the way. Elizabeth kept an eye on the fallen tree before her only stopping to glance up as the girls dramatically reached their arms out and called for help. About five feet from completing her mission, Elizabeth's foot slipped on some moss sending her tumbling to the ground in pain. It happened so quickly that she had no time to adjust her footing, causing her ankle to turn underneath her. She let out a muffled cry that sent the girls rushing to her side.

"Are you all right, Aunt Elizabeth?" questioned Sarah with worry.

"Yes, I think so," replied Elizabeth grasping hold of her pain filled ankle. "I twisted it that's all. I think it will be all right once I get up."

Sarah and Kate stood up and stepped back allowing their aunt room to stand. Elizabeth stood on her knees. She slowly brought her good foot up and rose to stand. It was more painful than she thought it would be, but at least she could stand. Now, if she could just make it out of the woods everything would be fine.

Chapter 11

Back at the house, Katherine noticed that Elizabeth and the girls had been gone for quite some time. She didn't want to disturb David's visit with John, but she felt someone needed to check on them. It was unusual for Elizabeth to be gone so long. Dirk had been outside most of the afternoon, maybe he had seen them. She decided to call him into the kitchen and ask. When Dirk told her he hadn't seen them, she was relieved that he volunteered to look for them.

In the woods, Elizabeth took one step forward with her good foot and carefully drug her injured foot into position beside the other one. She knew she was not moving very fast.

Sarah lost patience with the slow pace and suggested, "Maybe I could go on ahead and tell Pa what happened, and he could come for you."

"No," Elizabeth stated firmly. "Your Pa has company and I won't be interfering. He doesn't get to visit with old friends often. Besides, I don't want you trying to find your way back by yourself."

"Oh, all right," answered Sarah with disappointment.

Elizabeth knew the girls were getting tired, but she could do nothing about it. Her whole leg was aching, and she could feel that her ankle had swollen quite a bit. Feeling selfish, Elizabeth thought of how good it would feel if her brother would come and help her home.

Elizabeth, Kate, and Sarah trudged on. It seemed to take hours to accomplish any great distance. The girls continued to grow restless with the slow progress. Elizabeth had been tempted more than once to send Sarah on ahead, but her stubbornness and pride kept her from it.

All of the sudden Sarah piped up, "Did you hear that?"

"Don't try to scare your sister, Sarah," Elizabeth answered back. She was in no frame of mind to deal with Sarah's imagination.

"I'm not trying to scare anyone. I really heard something, didn't you?" she asked trying to plead her case. "Maybe someone is coming to find us."

"I'm sorry, Sarah, but I didn't hear anything," confessed Elizabeth.

"Wait!" Sarah persisted, putting up her hand to stop them from going further.

"All right we'll stop, but only for a few seconds then we need to keep moving," consented Elizabeth.

To be truthful, Elizabeth wanted nothing more than to sit down and rest. She knew the sun would be setting shortly, and it would be hard to see their way. Elizabeth concluded that the noise Sarah had heard was probably some squirrels or maybe a deer.

They all stood quietly waiting for the noise to reappear. When it did, they all became enthusiastic.

"I heard, I heard!" shouted Kate excitedly.

"Yes, I did too," agreed Elizabeth. "I'm sorry I doubted

you, Sarah. It does sound like someone walking through the woods over in that direction," Elizabeth pointed.

"Maybe it's Pa," exclaimed Kate.

Before Elizabeth had a chance to respond, Sarah gave a shout.

"Hello, is someone there?"

Then a familiar voice answered, "Sarah is that you?"

"It's Uncle Dirk," cried Sarah with excitement. "Uncle Dirk, we're over here!" She shouted and waved her arms up and down hoping he could see her. "Aunt Elizabeth's hurt," she added.

"Stay right where you are, I'm coming," reassured Dirk.

Even though it was Dirk that came, Elizabeth felt relief. She wondered why her brother sent Dirk. She didn't want to figure it out, so she sat down. In their merriment, the girls danced around in circles at the prospect of help on the way.

In the clearing up ahead, the girls saw Dirk heading in their direction. Sarah and Kate squealed with delight and ran to meet him. Elizabeth stayed put and watched the interaction between the threesome. The girls were obviously very fond of Dirk as they engulfed him with their hugs. The bright smile on his face reflected his adoration for them. Elizabeth watched as he put Kate upon his broad shoulders, and took hold of Sarah's hand so they could make their way in her direction.

Dirk sat Kate down on a nearby stump and knelt before Elizabeth. Before Elizabeth had a chance to utter a word, Dirk let her know about everyone's concern.

"Since John was still there, I volunteered to come."

Looking down quickly and shyly, Elizabeth answered, "Thank you."

With a mischievous grin on his face, Dirk spoke teasingly, "The girls tell me you were trying to rescue them from some wild beast. They said you almost fell into the ravine."

"Very funny," rebuked Elizabeth trying to stand up wincing in pain. "If you'll kindly help me up, I'll be on my way."

"Whoa, wait a minute," said Dirk gently helping Elizabeth back down. "You're not going anywhere until I get a look at that ankle."

Elizabeth reluctantly gave in, but pointed out, "It's not broken."

Dirk gently removed her shoe and saw the swollen ankle. After examining it the best he could, he announced, "It's badly sprained."

Without saying a word she looked him in the eye with her arms folded in front of her and a smile on her face.

"All right, I confess," he admitted. "You were right. But you need to stay off that foot."

Uncrossing her arms and placing them on her hips with her eyebrows furrowed she retorted, "And just how do you suggest that I get home?"

Now it was his turn to smile. He had her just where he wanted her. "I'm going to carry you. And don't argue with me on this one, Beth."

"All right," spoke Elizabeth in defeat. Her foot ached too much to argue. She never would have imagined that she would get back to the house in the arms of Dirk Hampton. Her mind went back to something he said. What had he called her? Maybe she had heard wrong.

Dirk was pleased that she hadn't put up a fuss. *She must be in quite a bit of pain to allow me to carry her*, he thought.

"I'll be as gentle as I can." He put one arm around her waist and the other under her knees beneath all the folds of her skirt. He rose to stand.

Elizabeth used her left arm and placed it around his shoulders for balance. She felt somewhat foolish and tried to dismiss the whole thing.

"Are you okay, Beth?"

Avoiding his gaze, she responded matter of fact, "Yes, I'm fine."

Dirk smiled down at Kate and Sarah who had been patiently

waiting. "Let's go girls. Your Ma and Pa will be glad to have the two of you back home."

Sarah grabbed a hold of Kate's hand as though she were in charge. "Come, Kate, let's go home."

As they walked, Dirk couldn't help but breathe in the scent of lilacs from Beth's hair. She smelled so good. He hoped that she couldn't feel the pounding of his heart. He studied the profile of her face in detail. To him, it was perfect. Dirk knew she was avoiding him. He also knew that she had swallowed her pride by allowing him to help her. He was surprised when she broke the silence.

"Why did you call me that?" asked Elizabeth defensively. She avoided looking at him directly.

Dirk wasn't exactly sure what she meant. "What did I call you?"

She turned and glared at him with disgust. "You don't know what you called me?"

She certainly got feisty when she was upset. He was tempted to call her the name of one of the young ladies in town, but he didn't want to risk her wrath. He spoke casually, "I called you Beth, is there something wrong with that?"

Dirk felt her body relax and wondered why she grew quiet.

Elizabeth's tone of voice softened as she answered, "It's just that you're the only one who's ever called me that beside my Pa."

Looking intently in her face, Dirk spoke out of concern. "I'll call you Elizabeth if that's what you want."

She hesitated and turned to meet his eyes. Speaking softly she answered, "No, Beth's fine."

In a whisper, for only her to hear, he said, "I'm glad."

Dirk's attention was soon diverted to young Kate who was tugging at his pant's leg. "Are we almost home?"

"Yes, Kate," he replied with a chuckle. "Do you see those two big pine trees up ahead?"

Kate and Sarah looked to where the trees stood.

"The yard is just beyond those trees," said Dirk.

"Yeah!" shouted the girls.

"Can we run ahead to tell Ma and Pa we're all right?" asked Sarah.

"Wait until we get to the trees. I don't want either of you to fall and get hurt," Dirk replied.

"Okay, Uncle Dirk," Sarah happily consented.

It was not too long before they came upon the two, large, pine trees. The house was in view. It was clearly visible that John and Melissa were gone. The girls gained renewed energy and took off running as fast as they could go. Both Dirk and Elizabeth laughed.

As Dirk and Elizabeth were nearing the house, Elizabeth spoke. "I want to thank you, Dirk. It seems like every time I turn around you're there to rescue me."

"You're welcome," grinned Dirk to make her feel at ease.

"I guess I should apologize for rushing off in town yesterday."

"You don't have to, Beth."

"Yes, I do," she sighed. "I would feel better if you knew the whole story."

"All right then, tell me," he prompted.

Elizabeth began, "John's family have been good friends of our family for many years." She hesitated before going on. "John and I were engaged to be married. We mutually broke the engagement a couple of months before the wedding. That's why I was so shocked to see him yesterday and to find out that he had married."

"I see," answered Dirk cautiously. "How do you feel about it now?"

"I'm better really," she responded with a half smile. "He's got a new life of his own, and I'm happy for him."

"Well, then," stated Dirk rather boldly not knowing how she would react. "Maybe you need to start a new beginning of your own."

Elizabeth broke into a full smile and looked happily into the eyes of Dirk Hampton. "I think I already have."

Chapter 12

Elizabeth was glad to have last weekend behind her. Last Sunday did have a positive side. Pastor Thompson announced a town social for the coming Sunday. It would be a fun event for everyone. Games would be played for all ages, and enough delicious food to satisfy everyone. For the married ladies, there would be a baked, pie contest. In Elizabeth's opinion, Katherine would take the blue ribbon. There was to be a lunch auction, for all of the eligible young ladies. Each young lady was to prepare a lunch for two and conceal the lunch in a decorated box. At noon each lunch would be auctioned off to the highest, eligible, gentleman bidder. He, in turn, would share the lunch with the girl who had prepared it. Elizabeth wasn't too keen on this part, but the money that was raised would go to buy much needed school supplies.

David hadn't needed her today, so she spent the day with

Katherine and the girls preparing for tomorrow's social. Elizabeth noticed that Katherine seemed to be tiring more easily these days. Katherine had only a few more weeks before the baby would come. When lunch time came, Elizabeth encouraged Katherine to lie down and rest. Elizabeth assured her that she would take care of the girls.

Elizabeth decided on a walk to the creek. Sarah and Kate picked wild flowers along the way. They were all having a good time together. Not long after they reached the creek, the girls begged their Aunt Elizabeth for permission to go wading. She approved and joined in the fun. They paraded around with glee in the knee-deep, crystal, clear water. They held their dresses up the best they could so as not to get them too wet.

After some time, they climbed up onto the grassy bank and sat down. It was a beautiful summer day. A cornflower blue sky with multitudes of puffy, cumulus clouds hung overhead. The trio lay on their backs gazing into the clouds for one that might take on the shape of an animal.

"Oh, look," began Sarah, proud to have found the first one. "There's a rabbit, see?" she exclaimed pointing her finger in the location. "The two clouds on top are the ears and the small one at the bottom is the tail."

"Yes, I see it," answered Elizabeth.

Elizabeth directed Kate toward the cloud. She was disappointed at not being able to locate it on her own. But her sadness was short lived as she shouted with glee! "I see the rabbit."

This game went on for several minutes until Sarah had a question for her aunt.

"Aunt Elizabeth, do you like Uncle Dirk?"

Elizabeth shot up to a sitting position at once. Dirk had received the honor of that name from her nieces because he frequented the Grafton house and was treated like family. He adored the girls. She couldn't blame them for making him a part, and she knew that she must choose her words carefully.

"Well, Dirk is a good friend to all of us, so I guess you could say that I like him."

"No, that's not what I mean," protested Sarah now sitting up. "Do you like him the way that Ma likes Pa?"

"You mean," Elizabeth hesitated. "Do I love him?"

"Yes, that's what I said," declared Sarah. "Do you?"

Oh, what this audacious five year old can come up with, thought Elizabeth. *Sarah is definitely one to speak her mind.*

Elizabeth tried her best to answer. "It's not that easy, Sarah, you have to..." stalled Elizabeth

"You have to what?" cut in Sarah.

"You have to have feelings for that person," continued Elizabeth not sure where this was leading. "When you love someone you want to spend the rest of your life with that person."

"Like Ma and Pa," declared Sarah.

"Yes," breathed Elizabeth with relief. Maybe she did understand. Changing the subject she announced, "We need to get our shoes back on and head back. Your Ma may need our help."

Both girls agreed, and set to work putting their stockings and shoes back on. Elizabeth finished quickly and helped Kate. She stood and reached down taking hold of each girls' hand, pulling them up to stand. The trio clasped hands and walked back to the house vibrantly soaking up the sunshine.

When they reached the house, Katherine was busily preparing for dinner and David was out in the barn.

Katherine secretively spoke to Elizabeth. "Someone was here asking about you."

"Who?" questioned Elizabeth with curiosity.

Before answering, Katherine turned towards the girls. "Why don't the two of you go out to the barn and see what your Pa is doing?"

Sarah and Kate didn't need to be told twice. They raced out the back door giggling with anticipation.

Very seldom did Katherine and Elizabeth get to have a conversation alone. Katherine had been wanting to speak with her. After the screen door closed, and Katherine knew that Sarah was out of ear shot she faced Elizabeth. With her hands on her hips and a mischievous smile across her face Katherine spoke. "Who else, Elizabeth would be asking of your whereabouts? Dirk of course."

"Well, what does he want with me?" asked Elizabeth innocently.

"I'm not for certain. He only said that he would come by later. I think he wants to escort you to the town social tomorrow," exclaimed Katherine with excitement.

"He can't," spoke Elizabeth quickly.

Katherine retorted back rather disturbed. "And why not?"

"He just can't that's all. I'll be taking care of the girls," argued Elizabeth.

"Nonsense," spoke Katherine in a somewhat scolding manner. "David and I will be attending the social. We'll look after the girls."

Elizabeth turned away and Katherine followed . She didn't normally pry into Elizabeth's life, but felt that her sister-in-law needed to have a good talk.

"What's the matter, Elizabeth?" questioned Katherine as she led Elizabeth by the hand to the table where they could sit down side by side. Katherine didn't waste words. "You have to know he has feelings for you, don't you?"

"I suppose maybe I do," she answered nervously.

"And do you have any for him?" questioned Katherine hoping Elizabeth would break down the emotional wall she had built between herself and everyone around her.

Elizabeth was on the verge of tears, and answered through trembling lips. "I...I don't know, Katherine, I'm confused. What if he's not the one for me either? I just don't want to go through that heart ache all over again." Once the words had escaped her lips the tears began to flow.

Katherine put her arm around Elizabeth and began. "Elizabeth, I know the decision to break off the engagement with John was not an easy one. But it seems like ever since then you've shut out anyone who wants to get close to you."

"Is it that obvious?" questioned Elizabeth drying the last tears from her cheeks.

"Not to everyone," admitted Katherine. "But I do know that David's been a little worried about you lately."

Elizabeth feeling emotionally depleted asked, "He has?"

"Yes," responded Katherine then cautiously continued. "Opening your heart, Elizabeth, is the only way to know your true feelings. I know you've prayed for God's direction, so let go and let God take control of the relationships in your life as well. Open your heart and I think you know where you stand with Dirk."

Elizabeth sank back in the chair and let Katherine's words soak in. "I don't know if I can do that. It's not going to be easy."

"Oh," assured Katherine. "I didn't say it would be easy. That's where your trust in the Lord comes in."

"I'll try, really I will," Elizabeth promised.

Elizabeth and Katherine ended their conversation with a hug and a prayer.

A knock on the door came during dinner, and Katherine flashed Elizabeth a smile. David looked at both of the women folk in his family and was curious as to what was going on between the two. In the mean time he got up to answer the door.

David was gone for only a short time when he rushed into the kitchen to grab his medical bag.

"What's the matter, David?" Katherine asked with worry.

"That was Dirk," he said quickly. "Jim Grayson and his boys were felling some trees when one landed on Jim. Dirk doesn't know any more than that."

Elizabeth got up from the table with concern and asked, "Is there anything I can do?"

"No, not right now. Just pray."

"We will," responded Katherine.

"I don't know when I'll be home, so don't wait up on me," he said as he bent over to give Katherine a kiss. As he hurried out the door where Dirk waited with the team, he called out over his shoulder, "You girls mind your Ma."

"Yes, Pa," the girls echoed in unison.

The evening dragged on slowly. Playing dolls with the girls didn't seem to make the time go any faster. After Katherine had finally tucked the girls into bed, she and Elizabeth sat and talked for a while before deciding to turn in for the night themselves.

Elizabeth lay in bed and couldn't sleep. Since her thoughts went to Mr. Grayson, she decided to pray for him again. Later, Dirk came to her mind. A smile spread across her face in the darkness as she remembered the first day they met. How kind and caring he had been. Katherine had been right. She had been afraid to love again. Lying there she prayed that God would give her wisdom to know what to do about Dirk.

Elizabeth couldn't remember when she fell asleep, but early morning she awakened to the sound of voices down stairs. Her brother must have returned home. She was anxious to hear about the condition of Mr. Grayson, but that would have to wait a few more hours. She yawned and rolled over to catch a couple more hours of sleep before dawn.

Chapter 13

Warm sunshine brought the start of another day. Katherine had informed Elizabeth about Mr. Grayson's several cracked ribs and broken leg. They chatted over a cup of coffee and a biscuit. The two women had begun filling the baskets with food for the social. Elizabeth had borrowed some pink ribbon from Katherine's sewing supplies to put the finishing touches on her boxed lunch.

David had slept in a little longer than usual due to his late night. He came out to the kitchen just as Elizabeth had finished her box. "What's that?" he questioned pointing to the box.

"A lunch," was all she replied.

"What's in it?" he asked amusingly.

"It's a surprise," responded Elizabeth running out of patience.

David remarked teasingly, "I sure wouldn't want to buy something I didn't know I was eating."

"Oh, David, you're impossible," proclaimed his sister. "I'm just kidding you know. It looks real nice, Sis, I'm sure it will take top dollar. All the young men will be jumping at the chance to eat lunch with you," added David with confidence.

"We're never going to finish with you in here, joked Katherine through a smile. "Don't you have anything to do?"

"All right," said David throwing up his hands in surrender. "I can take a hint. I'll be out in the barn. A man can't even have a cup of coffee in his own house," he added tauntingly before going out the door.

Katherine and Elizabeth looked at one another and broke into laughter.

Suddenly the laughter stopped. Katherine gasped as a sharp pain streaked through her abdomen. She took her place quickly in a nearby chair.

Elizabeth startled by this sudden reaction, quickly sat her things down and went to her sister-in-law. "Katherine, what's wrong?"

"It's just a contraction," responded Katherine.

"But the baby isn't due for another couple of weeks," stated Elizabeth with worry.

Katherine being experienced at giving birth responded calmly. "Babies come when they want to come. They're not on a time schedule."

Feeling a little more at ease, but still cautious, Elizabeth asked, "Do you want me to get David?"

"No, don't bother him, I'm sure it's nothing to be concerned about right now," insisted Katherine rising to her feet. "The girls will be up soon. I need to start their breakfast."

"Let me do it," Elizabeth pleaded as she put aside what she was doing.

Complying with Elizabeth, Katherine spoke, "All right if it will make you feel better. I'll just go see about getting the girls ready." She left the kitchen without expressing her own uneasiness. By the baby's position, Katherine hoped that the baby would not come. She had assisted David in enough births to know the possible danger.

As Sarah and Kate came bounding into the kitchen, Elizabeth had just finished their eggs. The town social was an exciting time for them as well. They were looking forward to a time of fun with their friends.

Katherine followed the girls with a pained expression on her face. She didn't want to cause alarm to the girls. Quietly she called Elizabeth over to her and spoke in a whisper. "Elizabeth, please go and get David."

Elizabeth responded in alarm, "What's wrong?"

"I'm not sure at this point. I would just like him to check the baby."

"All right," said Elizabeth. She turned to face the girls. "I'm going out to see your Pa and tell him breakfast is ready. You girls stay in here with your Ma." Before leaving, she looked to Katherine for approval.

David came immediately. It was just as Katherine hoped wouldn't happen, the baby was on the way. David's heart ached for his wife. He knew this was going to be a hard delivery with the baby not in the birthing position.

There was a knock at the door; it was Dirk. Elizabeth bid him to come in and sit down. The girls were just finishing up their breakfast. She offered him a cup of coffee, which he readily accepted.

Coming from the bedroom where Katherine rested, David acknowledged Dirk's presence. Giving Sarah and Kate a half smile he announced, "Girls, your Ma is going to have our new baby today."

They giggled and shouted with glee. "When, Pa, when?" asked Sarah.

"Well," David explained. "Babies take time. Remember, Sarah, when you spent the night with the Allen's when Kate was born?"

"Yes," Sarah nodded. She liked the Allen's. Their daughter, Polly was her age. "Do we get to spend the night there?"

"I don't know yet," spoke David gently. "But here's what I want you to do." Looking to Dirk and hoping he would agree, he told the girls that Dirk would take them to the social. "There Mrs. Allen will take care of you. If the baby still hasn't come by the end of the social, you are to go home with the Allen's until I come for you. Does that sound okay?"

"Okay," said Sarah happily. She was glad that she would not miss the social. Plus she would have a new baby afterwards.

"What about you, pumpkin?" David asked as he picked Kate up and lifted her high into the air.

"Okay," said Kate mimicking her sister.

Relieved, David kissed Kate on the forehead and sat her back down. He helped Dirk load the wagon for the town social, along with Elizabeth's decorated lunch for the auction. David was sorry Elizabeth would miss the social, but he would need her help.

Dirk watched as Elizabeth braided the girls' hair. He knew she was doing her best to make them feel happy, so they wouldn't worry about their Ma. He couldn't help but feel a little disappointed at not being able to take Elizabeth, but he would do as David had asked.

After the wagon was loaded, David lifted the girls up giving each one a kiss before placing them on the seat "Have a good time today," he encouraged them. Turning to Dirk he spoke. "Thank you. I appreciate you doing this for us. I know you had other plans. I'll make it up to you," said David looking in Elizabeth's direction.

"Glad to be of help, David," replied Dirk. "Let me know if there's anything more I can do."

David nodded in response. He waved to the girls before going back inside the house.

Taking Elizabeth's hands in his, Dirk spoke tenderly and quietly, "Beth."

Her heart quickened. Elizabeth hadn't heard him call her that since the day she sprained her ankle. She could tell by the sound of his voice he was sincere.

"Katherine is going to be just fine. She's strong; she'll make it."

Elizabeth gazed into Dirk's eyes. His closeness conjured up feelings she hadn't felt for along time. Was it love she felt for this man? Now, was not the time to sort out her feelings. Katherine mattered now. "Pray, Dirk, please," she pleaded serenely.

"I will," he spoke as he brought her hands up to his and kissed them softly. "That's a promise." After releasing her hands slowly, he climbed up into the wagon "Ready to go, ladies?" he asked the girls.

"Ready, Uncle Dirk," replied Sarah and Kate in chorus.

"Good bye, Aunt Elizabeth," waved Sarah. "I wish you were coming with us."

Waving in return she replied, "Have fun!"

Calling over his shoulder Dirk spoke, "Don't worry I'll buy your lunch, Beth, but you have to promise me that you'll share it with me later."

How could she refuse? "I promise," she called out with a smile to match his. Turning she went into the house with a bounce in her step.

The morning turned into late afternoon and Katherine's contractions still weren't regular. David and Elizabeth tried to keep her as comfortable as possible.

Later, Elizabeth was out in the kitchen making Katherine some cool sassafras tea. She had been praying for Katherine and the baby when David stepped out demanding her presence.

"Elizabeth," he spoke firmly. "It's time, I need to try to turn the baby."

She stopped what she was doing and went immediately.

Elizabeth didn't know how long it took, but was relieved to finally see the look of stress lift from her brother's face. He had been successful. Within the hour, David Andrew Grafton entered the world healthy as could be.

Elizabeth cleaned and wrapped him in a soft, cotton blanket. She laid him in Katherine's outstretched arms. Tears of joy welled up in her eyes as she held her baby boy. Leaving David, Katherine, and their new son to get acquainted, Elizabeth quietly slipped from the room.

Several hours later, David brought the girls home. They were so excited to see their new baby brother. Katherine was propped up in bed with little David in her arms. Sarah and Kate clamored up on the bed to get a better look.

"He's so small," Sarah commented.

"You were just as small when you were born," explained Katherine.

"I was?" asked Sarah in disbelief. She took hold of his small hand.

Wondering for a moment at this small brother of hers, Kate asked, "Can he play with me?"

"Not yet, sweetheart," smiled Katherine. "He has to get bigger before he can play. For now he will just eat and sleep."

Kate expressed to everyone that she thought that would be no fun. She gave her Ma a kiss and slipped down from the bed and went to find her doll.

The girls were already for bed. In the excitement over their new brother, they forgot to tell about their fun at the social. Sarah, being the oldest did most of the talking to their aunt. She told of the fun games, the food, and how Uncle Dirk ate lunch with Mary Collins,

Sitting on the edge of the bed, Elizabeth listened without interruption until Sarah mentioned Dirk. Letting her curiosity get the best of her, Elizabeth questioned Sarah. "Did Dirk buy Mary Collins' lunch?"

"He sure did," stated Sarah with pride for knowing. "He

sat right down under a big tree and ate it with her. Her box was pretty too. You should have seen it, Aunt Elizabeth."

"I'm sure it was, Sarah," replied Elizabeth heartbroken. Changing the subject, she went on to speak. "Well, girls, it's time for you to get some sleep. Your Pa will be in to give you a kiss." Before leaving, she covered them up and gave each one a kiss and announced, "Sweet dreams."

Elizabeth went directly to her room. It had been a long day. Despite the joy of seeing her little nephew come into the world, she had a heavy heart. Her thoughts turned to Dirk as she climbed into bed. *How could he share a lunch with Mary after he promised me?* She had finally begun to allow her feelings to follow the path of love once again, only to be betrayed. Trying to reason with herself she thought, *maybe there was some misunderstanding. Maybe Sarah's wrong. No, she said they were eating together. Sarah even described Mary's box in detail. I'll just confront him and see if he denies* it, she decided. *How else can I know the truth?* She blew out the lantern and fell asleep under exhaustion and tears.

Chapter 14

For the past few weeks, Elizabeth had been busy taking over most of Katherine's household chores since the baby had arrived. David had relieved her of her office duties for a while. Sarah and Kate weren't too happy with the arrangements because it left less time for their aunt to spend with them. Elizabeth's schedule also left her little time to think on Dirk, whom she hadn't seen except on Sundays at church.

Before lunch time, Elizabeth hung out the last of the laundry. With the sultry, July weather, it wouldn't take them long to dry. At least a slight breeze blew today. Yesterday had been almost unbearable.

Picking up the clothes basket, Elizabeth headed toward the house. She heard a wagon approaching. Looking up, she shielded the sun from her eyes with her hand to get a better look. It was Dirk. *What was he doing here,* she thought.

Before Elizabeth could get into the house, Dirk called her name. Ignoring Dirk entered her mind, but he would only follow her inside. Besides, maybe an emergency came up and David needed her help.

Dirk jumped down from the wagon and ran to catch up to her before she disappeared inside.

"Hello, Beth," he said hardly able to contain his excitement.

"What are you doing here?" she asked out of curiosity. "Shouldn't you be at the office or visiting your patients?"

"What patients? What office? I completely forgot about them," he answered sarcastically.

"But since I'm here now, how would you like to go on a picnic?" he asked out of sheer delight.

Elizabeth just shook her head, rolled her eyes, and put on half a grin. Dirk could be such a tease. She sat the clothes basket down, put her hands on her hips, and looked him straight in the eye and asked, "Dirk, what are you talking about?"

Keeping with his jovial mood he answered, "Oh, I thought I just told you. I've come to take you on a picnic."

"Does my brother know that you are out and about making a fool of yourself?" she questioned with a bit of sarcastic humor.

Thinking she was just about hooked, Dirk answered in a serious tone. "Yes, I told him I had an important appointment this afternoon. He told me to have a good time." He winked, smiled, and tipped his hat all in one motion. "Now, can we go on that picnic? I'm starved."

Elizabeth retrieved her laundry basket and replied as she turned to go into the house. "I can't I don't have anything prepared for a picnic."

"Wait," he called out jumping in front and blocking her way. "Wait just one minute," he pleaded holding up one finger. "Close your eyes."

"What? Close my eyes? Dirk, I don't have time for games," she replied half serious.

Dirk took the basket from her hands and put it aside. "Just close your eyes, Beth, it's a surprise."

Knowing she would soon lose the argument, she consented with a sigh. "All right, Dirk, but please hurry I don't have all day."

Dirk ran over to the wagon and picked up something. But before he turned around with it he asked, "Are your eyes closed?"

Feeling completely vulnerable she answered, "Yes, they're closed."

"Good," said Dirk. "And no peeking."

He walked over to where Elizabeth stood, and prayed that someday she would be his.

Interrupting his mind full of thoughts about her, Elizabeth asked, "Can I open them now?"

"Yes, you can." After Elizabeth opened her eyes, he called out, "Surprise!"

Elizabeth's eyes opened to something covered up with a blanket. She was not sure how to respond, so she carefully asked, "What is it?"

"A picnic lunch fit for a king and queen," he said with pride as he pulled the blanket off revealing Elizabeth's auctioned box.

Taken completely by surprise, she didn't know what to say. Dirk held her box wrapped exactly as she had it for the auction.

"I don't understand," she muttered.

Gratified to know he had surprised her, Dirk went on to explain. "I told you I would buy your lunch, Beth, and I did. I knew you would be busy with Katherine and the new baby coming and all, so I took it home later that day and ate it by myself."

"You didn't share it with Mary Collins?" she asked reservedly.

Now growing serious, Dirk set the lunch down and took

Elizabeth's hands. He looked longingly into her eyes and answered, You are the only one I would share it with."

Returning his gaze, she overwhelmingly expressed, "Oh, Dirk."

After a moments time, Dirk released her hands and asked grinning, "Now, Miss Grafton, would you do me the honor of a picnic?"

Elizabeth reciprocated his smile and replied, "Yes, Mr. Hampton, I'd be delighted." But reality soon came to her. She had forgotten about her duties. Elizabeth turned to Dirk. Her face was covered with disappointment. "I'm sorry, I can't, Dirk. I forgot about the girls. I did tell Katherine I would look after them."

Not missing a beat Dirk replied, "That's all been arranged. We're taking them with us. I worked out the details with David yesterday. It's not quite what I had in mind, but at least I'll get to spend some time with you."

Elizabeth smiled at him for his thoughtfulness. He had thought of everything. But out of curiosity she asked, "How did you know I would say yes?"

"Ah, my lady," he spoke in disguise. "That is a secret to which I alone have the answer."

Pushing him away teasingly, she picked up her laundry basket and went into the house with Dirk at her heels.

The girls were excited to be going on a picnic. Sarah was curious as to what they were going to eat. She hadn't seen her aunt prepare anything. Dirk explained that since he wasn't much of a cook he had asked Mrs. Flanagan at the boarding house to fix them a lunch. He asked her to prepare the exact same lunch that Elizabeth had made for the social.

Elizabeth couldn't believe Dirk had gone to so much trouble. She was curious to know what Mrs. Flanagan thought of his request.

"She was happy to do it," he replied. "She told me it was about time I think of settling down. She told me that you would make a fine choice of a girl to court," he added teasingly.

Elizabeth's cheeks flushed with embarrassment. "She did not," she argued.

"Yes, she did," Dirk stated. "And as for the courting part, I think I'll get started on it right away," he winked. "Let's get going on that picnic."

"Yeah!" shouted the girls jumping up and down. They were not quite sure what had just transpired in their kitchen between these two people they loved, but they knew it was good.

Down by the creek under a thriving Maple tree, Elizabeth spread the blanket that Dirk had provided. Mrs. Flanagan had done a fine job preparing their lunch. She would be sure to thank her come Sunday.

The girls were hungry and ate heartily. Everything was delicious right down to the blackberry pie. The cool refreshing ice tea quenched everyone's thirst. No sooner had the girls finished eating, they wanted to go wading in the creek.

Dirk readily agreed of course and began removing his shoes. "Last one in gets tickled," he urged.

That sent Kate and Sarah into a giggling frenzy as they each tried not to be last.

Elizabeth sat watching in amusement.

Dirk glanced toward Elizabeth. "That goes for you too, you know."

"Me?" she asked completely caught off guard.

"It goes double for you so you had better get to unlacing those shoes," Dirk taunted.

After Dirk had finished, he helped the girls. Elizabeth knew that she didn't stand a chance no matter how fast she tried.

Dirk, Kate, and Sarah proclaimed Elizabeth the last one. She felt like a trapped animal. The girls circled her, then in utter delight they began to dish out the consequences.

Elizabeth laughed until she could bear it no more. Dirk just sat there and enjoyed the whole scene until she called for him.

"Did I hear a call for help," he teased. "Why it's a damsel in distress." He scooped Elizabeth up in his arms and took her down to the creek.

"Thank you, my knight in shining armor," she continued in the scheme of things.

Putting her down gently to stand in the creek, he responded, "You are quite welcome."

Time passed by with splashing and picking up of shiny, smooth stones. But Sarah soon became tired of wading and suggested a game of tag. They ran and chased after one another through the tall grass until they were exhausted. Everyone collapsed on the blanket and enjoyed another refreshing drink of ice tea.

After their drink, the girls went to pick wild flowers for their Ma. Dirk and Elizabeth sat quietly watching Kate and Sarah for a few moments then simultaneously their eyes fastened on each other.

Wanting to ask Dirk about the social, she became nervous. She wanted to know the truth. One part of her wanted to forget the whole thing, but the other part of her needed to know. She gathered her boldness about her and plunged ahead. "Dirk, I have something to ask you. I know this may sound foolish, but I want to know the truth ."

Dirk sensing that she was uneasy and concerned declared, "Go ahead, ask me."

She bit her lip, a habit she had whenever she was nervous, but went forward. "A few weeks ago at the town social did you buy Mary Collins' lunch?"

He was relieved to know that it wasn't anything serious. He simply stated, "Yes, I did." Dirk could tell Elizabeth was tensing up, so he spoke up. "Now, you wanted to know the truth so just hear me out, all right?"

Dirk explained that he had bought Elizabeth's lunch first.

Hers had sold for the highest amount. After that, he planned on leaving but decided to stay and see just how much money the school would raise. Dirk told her how Mary's lunch happened to be the last box to be auctioned off. He bid only because Harold Watts was the only bidder. He didn't want Mary's lunch to go for nearly nothing. So, he bid to up the price. Just when he dropped out of the bidding, Harold quit his bid. "And that left me buying Mary's lunch. That's the truth," he finished.

"Thanks for telling me. I'm sorry I doubted you," she apologized.

"I planned on telling you the day of the social, but I didn't get a chance. That's one reason I wanted to bring you here today so we could talk. We haven't done much of that lately," he finished in earnest.

Feeling ashamed, she looked downward toward the blanket and whispered softly, "I know." Not wanting to ruin a perfectly good day, she looked up slowly with a smile and added, "Dirk, I want to thank you for today. It's been absolutely wonderful."

Moving over closer to Elizabeth, he looked down into her soft, delicate face and emerald green eyes and whispered for her only, "You're welcome. Just promise me that you'll come again just you and me."

Looking at him with affection, she whispered, "I promise."

Once again he was so near to her he breathed in the fragrance of lilacs from her hair. He longed to take her in his arms. All at once the spark that held them both suddenly broke by two very hot and tired girls who plopped down on the blanket in front of them.

Everyone had one more glass of tea before packing up and heading home. Sarah and Kate couldn't wait to get home to tell their Ma of the fun they had. Sarah chattered nonstop until they reached the house. Dirk and Elizabeth occasionally got in a word or two, but they always managed to communicate to each other with a smile.

Dropping Elizabeth and the girls off, Dirk went on his way.

He had promised David that he would help with routine check ups.

Katherine listened intently to the talk of her daughters. Sarah told in detail the events of the afternoon. She even mentioned Dirk and Elizabeth.

"You should have seen them, Ma. They whispered and told secrets," Sarah mentioned in excitement.

"Is that so?" Katherine questioned as she glanced toward Elizabeth who's face was flushed three shades of pink. Katherine laughed softly. She was glad things were working out for Elizabeth and Dirk. She looked again at Elizabeth who this time was beaming with happiness. Katherine asked, "So, Elizabeth, it sounds like you've decided to open you heart after all. Any regrets?"

Elizabeth couldn't help but smile in thankfulness for her and Katherine's talk they had. And without hesitation she answered, "No, regrets."

Chapter 15

"Step right up to get your very own copy of the *Times Reporter*. Read about your own newspaper coming soon to Dover," yelled a man standing in the center of the street.

Elizabeth had heard the commotion and stepped out of the general store to see what it was all about.

"One penny is all it costs to read the *Times Reporter*. One round penny to find out about your neighboring Stark County and to read about your very own up and coming newspaper," yelled the man.

Elizabeth watched as people purchased the papers scouring the news of Canton. She moved closer to get a better view.

This man, who was dressed in a very neat, navy blue, pin stripped suit, removed the canvas that covered a large wooden sign. In big, bold, black letters it read, Coming Soon the *Dover Chronicle*, published by Philip Morgan. Elizabeth

turned to leave just as this newcomer caught her attention.
"Excuse me, Miss. With whom do I have the pleasure of speaking?"

Elizabeth felt somewhat embarrassed for having been chosen out of the crowd like that. She hesitated before answering. "Elizabeth Grafton, sir."

"Oh, what a beautiful name for a beautiful lady." And he took Elizabeth's hand and kissed it in a gentlemanly fashion. "May I introduce myself? I am Philip Morgan."

"So, you are the one who's going to run the newspaper," declared Elizabeth.

"I am indeed, the very one. Philip Morgan at your service," he stated tipping his hat.

Elizabeth felt flattered by his speech. She did not want to appear without manners herself so she went on to say, "It's nice to meet you, Mr. Morgan, welcome to Tuscarawas County."

"Please call me Philip. And thank you, Elizabeth. It is all right if I call you by your first name isn't it?" he questioned cautiously. "I like first names better. It gives one a sense of belonging."

Elizabeth was taken back by his boldness, but she did want him to feel welcome. "Yes, Elizabeth's fine."

"Good!" he exclaimed beaming with a grin from ear to ear. "I know we've just met, but it seems like we've known each other all our lives," he proclaimed in an upbeat manner. "I am sure we are going to be very good friends." Looking around as the crowd had dispersed, he turned toward Elizabeth once more. "Now, would you be so kind to direct me to the boarding house. For the present time, that is where I shall be staying."

"Of course," obliged Elizabeth pointing him in the right direction before she herself turned to leave. "If you'll excuse me, Mr. Morgan."

"Philip," he cut her off and corrected. "Please call me Philip."

Elizabeth started again. This time remembering to call him

by his first name. "If you'll excuse me, Philip, I need to be getting home."

"Oh, certainly and thank you again for your help," he said smiling in appreciation. But before she turned to leave he spoke up once more. "I hope we will meet again soon, Elizabeth."

Elizabeth didn't exactly know why, but she spoke up rather boldly herself. "I'll be in church tomorrow."

Philip was not a regular church attendee, but he could be easily persuaded when in the presence of a beautiful woman such as Elizabeth.

Taking the red, rose bud from his lapel, he bowed and presented it to Elizabeth. "Until tomorrow then my beautiful rose."

Elizabeth accepted the rose instinctively and excused herself. She left, leaving Philip Morgan standing in the street watching after her until she was out of his sight.

On the walk home, Elizabeth thought about her meeting with Philip Morgan. He certainly was intriguing. A very dashing gentleman at that. His jet, black hair parted on one side fell down onto his forehead when he removed his hat. Elizabeth was impressed by his dress as well as his positive outlook. It suited him. It would be nice to have a newspaper in their very own town. She was sure Dirk would like him too. They both looked to be about the same age, and they were both staying at the boarding house. She would be sure to mention Philip to everyone at dinner this evening.

The girls were waiting for her outside when Elizabeth got home. Since Katherine had dinner pretty well in hand, Elizabeth went outside and pushed the girls in the swing until it was time to eat.

Dinner conversation started out light and minimal until David brought up the subject of the newspaper.

"You should have heard the commotion around town today. Everyone was talking about Dover getting their own newspaper," he announced scoffing.

"I think it would be a wonderful thing," proclaimed Katherine in excitement. "To read news from our own community. But you don't sound very excited, David."

"Yes, and no," he wavered. "Newspapers can be a good thing unless put into the hands of the wrong journalist. When I was in Medical School in Chicago, I would read the paper once in a while and so many of the articles had a twisted view."

"Well, added Elizabeth defensively. "I don't think that will happen here. This isn't the big city."

"I hope you're right, Elizabeth. The talk around town is that this newspaper journalist came in on the train today. I wouldn't mind meeting him just to talk with him and find out more about this newspaper."

Elizabeth blurted out, "You can; he'll be in church tomorrow."

David and Katherine were both taken by surprise to know how Elizabeth knew this information.

Katherine spoke first. "How did you know this man will be in church tomorrow?"

Knowing her brother's opinion of newspaper journalists, Elizabeth didn't know how her brother would react. David would just have to meet him and see for himself that Philip isn't at all like those Chicago journalists. With her mind made up, she answered Katherine's question. "I happened to be in town when he unveiled the sign bearing the announcement of the coming newspaper. He introduced himself as Philip Morgan. I wanted him to feel welcome to the community, so I invited him to church."

"That was a kind thing to do, Elizabeth," said Katherine sympathetically.

David trying to look out for his sister cautioned, "Just be careful, Sis."

"I'm perfectly capable of taking care of myself, David. There's no need to worry. He's just a journalist not a bank robber." Elizabeth knew she shouldn't be so harsh, but after all she was a grown woman.

Katherine decided to ease the situation by coming up with a favorably proposition. "Why don't we invite Mr. Morgan over to dinner after church tomorrow. That way we can get acquainted and, David, you can talk to him about his paper."

"Oh, Katherine, that's a wonderful idea," exclaimed Elizabeth. She knew Katherine would see things her way. Men were sometimes so exasperating.

David hesitated looking first to his wife then to his sister. He wasn't too sure about this, but decided to give the man the benefit of the doubt. "All right I'll invite him."

Elizabeth could hardly wait for Dirk to get there. They had been taking walks in the evening. She had thoroughly enjoyed them. She learned so much more about Dirk. His mother and younger sister still lived in Colorado. He had told her about his father's tragic accident while working on the railroad. If Dirk would have been able to get him to a doctor, he might still be alive today. That's one of the reasons Dirk chose to become a doctor.

Elizabeth was sitting on the porch when he arrived. She couldn't wait to tell him about the town newspaper. She hoped he wouldn't be as stubborn about it as David had been.

Dirk rode up to the back fence and tethered Doc, his horse. Elizabeth ran to meet him in eagerness.

"Hi, Beth, it's so nice to know that you miss me so much that you run to meet me," he teased.

"Oh, Dirk, I am glad to see you, but I wanted to tell you the exciting news," she exclaimed excitedly.

"Well, what is it?" he questioned with anticipation.

"Dover is going to have their very own newspaper," she chattered. I met Philip in town today. I invited him to church tomorrow, and David is going to ask him to come to dinner after church."

"Whoa! Slow down, Beth," stated Dirk raising both hands

up in the air. "One thing at a time. And go a little slower. I caught the part about the paper. I heard that in town today. Now what's this about inviting Philip to church and dinner? Philip who?"

"Oh, I'm sorry I went so fast," Elizabeth apologized. "I am just so excited. You see Philip is the newspaper journalist. He's staying at the boarding house. I met him this afternoon, and David's inviting him to have dinner with us tomorrow."

"Is this Philip a member of the family or something?" He asked out of a sense of inquisitiveness.

"No, of course not, Dirk," stated Elizabeth. "I told you I just met him today."

"And you're on a first name basis with him already?" questioned Dirk a little disturbed.

This was not going the way Elizabeth hoped it would, so she answered carefully. "Well, yes, he said he preferred first names. It gives him a sense of belonging," she finished by biting her lip. "I thought you would be excited about having a newspaper. You're reacting just like David."

"What do you mean? If David's not for sure about this newspaper man, then why is he inviting him to dinner?" asked Dirk getting a little confused.

"So we can welcome him to the community and get acquainted before everyone goes judging him," exclaimed Elizabeth in a rather sharp tone of voice.

Dirk took a deep breath. He realized that he had reacted too abruptly, so he apologized. "Look, Beth, I'm sorry. I didn't mean to upset you. This is not how I wanted our evening to be."

"I know. Neither did I," spoke Elizabeth softly. She was sorry she brought up the subject. She had no idea it would cause such a reaction. "I'm sorry too. I just hoped you would be as happy as I was when I heard the news."

Dirk didn't have any objections to a newspaper; it was this Philip he wasn't so sure about He decided to try to ease things a little. "I am happy about the newspaper really, but can we forget it for now and talk about something else?" he requested.

"All right," Dirk, she quietly consented.

"Good," he spoke as he took her hand in his and began walking.

Their walk ended much shorter than it usually did. Neither one of them could think of much to talk about other than the progress of various patients. Dirk didn't linger long after their walk either. He dismissed himself saying that he had a busy day and was tired. Elizabeth stood on the porch step and watched him mount his horse.

Before riding away, Dirk spoke trying to muster enthusiasm. "I'll pick you up for church tomorrow all right?"

"Yes, Dirk, that will be fine. Good night," she called out, disheartened.

"Good night," he returned.

Elizabeth went into the house feeling discouraged. What she had meant for happiness had caused tension between them. She didn't understand that was for sure. Maybe Dirk was just tired this evening like he said. Trying to lift her spirits she thought, *everything will be fine tomorrow. After David and Dirk meet Philip they'll see that I was right. Everything will work out all right, I hope.*

Chapter 16

Philip graciously accepted the invitation for Sunday dinner. They all learned that afternoon the newspaper had really been owned by Philip's father. Philip revealed that since the newspaper had done so well in Canton, his father decided to branch out into other communities. His printing press and other equipment would be arriving on Monday's train. Knowing that her brother and Dirk were not too keen on Philip, it surprised her when they offered Philip their services. The men would help unload the boxcar containing everything Philip would need to start the coming newspaper. Threatening rain clouds compelled Dirk and Philip to leave the Grafton house sooner than either one had anticipated.

By morning, the town had received an ample amount of rainfall. The rain had cooled things down a bit causing it to be less humid. There were puddles scattered throughout the garden. Elizabeth enjoyed walking barefoot letting the mud ooze through her toes.

Since David was helping Philip this morning, he didn't need her until late afternoon. She spent the morning with Sarah and Kate. Elizabeth found pleasure in watching the girls race through the puddles. Their shrieks of delight could be heard for quite a distance she was sure.

Making their way back to the house, Sarah and Kate walked on each side of Elizabeth. They heard a horse approaching. Elizabeth wasn't quite sure who it was. As the figure got closer, she could tell that it was David, but why did he have Dirk's horse?

"Elizabeth!" he called out.

"What's the matter, has something happened to Dirk?" she questioned running to greet him.

"No, Dirk, is fine. I need for you and Katherine to help me move things out of the back room," he answered as he dismounted the horse. "I'll tell you both everything once I've stabled Doc."

Nodding in relief over Dirk's well being, she took the girls into the house while David led Dirk's horse to the barn.

Elizabeth and Katherine had already begun cleaning things out of the spare room when David came to help.

Katherine and Elizabeth stopped what they were doing. Katherine spoke first. "David, what's going on?"

"Well, it happened this morning as Dirk and I were helping Philip. We had just about everything unloaded. Phillip insisted on carrying the crate that held his typewriter. When he went to step down off the boxcar, he slipped in the mud and his left leg twisted underneath him. He broke his leg," David explained.

"Oh, no," sighed Katherine.

"Poor Philip," chimed in Elizabeth. "But what's the room for?"

"I was getting to that," replied David. "Philip sustained a pretty bad break. I had to cast the whole leg. I hope you don't mind, Katherine, but I told Philip that he could stay here with us for a while until he's able to move around on his own. There is no foreseeable way that he could stay at the boarding house with all of those steps. He has no family to see to his needs."

"Yes, by all means. He's welcome to stay for as long as it takes," sympathized Katherine.

"I thought you might feel that way," smiled David. "There will be some inconveniences though. With Dirk and myself in town a good part of the day, that will leave Mr. Morgan's care up to the two of you."

"We'll manage just fine," assured Katherine. "Won't we Elizabeth?"

"Yes," confirmed Elizabeth. "You have nothing to worry about."

"Good," exclaimed David relieved. "It's a good thing we have a spare bed already in here. Dirk will be here any time with Philip. Katherine, if you could see to getting a couple of extra pillows. Elizabeth, if You'll get the oil lamp off the mantle and bring it in here; this room will be just about ready. It won't be fancy, but our patient should be comfortable."

As soon as everything had been put in order, the sound of approaching wagon wheels could be heard. Dirk pulled the wagon as close as he could to the house. David went outside to assist Dirk. Katherine held the door while David and Dirk carried him in on a slab of wood. The slab steadied Philip and helped reduce discomfort. Dirk issued Philip more laudanum before the trip to keep him sedated. Elizabeth brought in Philip's traveling case that Dirk retrieved from the boarding house. It was filled with necessities. Looking on, Kate and Sarah hoped that they could share in the duties of tending to Mr. Morgan. The thought of having one of their Pa's patients staying in their house proved to be one of interest.

Dirk and David stayed to eat lunch before heading back to town. David instructed Katherine and Elizabeth about Philip's care. "I've given him some medication which should cause him to sleep for several hours. If he should wake and become restless, you may give him more. I want him to sleep as much as possible. He needs to keep that leg still," David instructed.

"Don't worry about a thing, David," said Katherine smiling to her husband.

Before David left, he held his little son who had just wakened from a nap. He kissed his daughters and Katherine before heading out the door.

Dirk had already gone out to the barn to saddle Doc. Elizabeth hurried out to follow him. She didn't want him to leave until she had a chance to talk with him. She knew their conversation on Saturday had been strained, and she missed yesterdays walk tremendously. It would be another whole week before they would have time together again.

Elizabeth quietly walked into the barn and spoke, "Hello, Dirk."

Elizabeth startled his thoughts. He was thinking about the situation with Philip at the Grafton house. It bothered him that Philip Morgan would be so near Elizabeth . Philip Morgan couldn't be trusted. His cheesy smile and persuasive speech made his skin crawl. Turning around, he answered her, "Hello, Beth. Do you need a ride into town? We could both ride Doc," he winked.

"I've got to stay here, remember?"

"How could I forget," he retorted smugly. "I was just trying to be cheerful about the whole thing."

"Oh, Dirk, you have nothing to worry about. Besides, I have a request to make," she added teasingly.

He moved over closer to her. "And what would that be?" he asked in seriousness.

Dirk's mood changed when she looked up into his eyes as she gently spoke. "I want you to come for dinner this evening. I know you usually don't come during the week, but you and I can spend some time together. I missed our walk yesterday, Dirk."

Whenever she looked up at him like that and spoke softly, he found it hard to deny her anything. "I'll be there," he promised. "I missed having you all to myself yesterday."

Her heart quickened when he took her hand in his and gently drew her to himself. The scent of lilacs would carry him through his day. Brushing her forehead with a kiss, he slowly released her and whispered, "I'll see you tonight." Dirk walked out of the barn and mounted his horse.

"Bye," she called out smiling and waving.

The day went fairly smooth as Katherine and Elizabeth went about the house hold chores and saw to the needs of the children. Elizabeth hung out the laundry, while Katherine swept the floors. They both kept a close eye on their patient. Katherine and Elizabeth spent much time in the kitchen making bread and blackberry pies. They started dinner preparations when they heard stirring coming from the spare room. Elizabeth went in to check and make sure everything was all right.

Philip had stirred to awareness. He smiled when he saw Elizabeth. "Oh, my sweet nurse."

"How are you feeling, Philip?" she asked checking his temperature.

"My leg aches terribly," he proclaimed. "Is this your brother's house?"

"Yes, but you need to rest now. Do you want some water?" she asked pouring some into a cup.

With a nod of his head, he closed his eyes. Gently holding up his head with one hand, she held the cup to his mouth with the other. He took a few sips. She gave him more laudanum and within a few minutes, sleep overcame him.

With dinner ready, Elizabeth, Katherine, and the girls waited and waited. It happened sometimes with David being a doctor. In the meantime, Katherine fed and changed little David's diaper. The girls became antsy, so Elizabeth decided to play a game of jacks with them. About an hour later, both men came in the door. After everyone had been seated and the blessing said, David explained to Katherine and Elizabeth why they were late. He told them that while Dirk got called away to the Eckert's home, Mr. Hentzel rushed into the office saying his wife was about to give birth to their fourth child. Dirk shared his experience of riding nearly three miles out of town to the Eckert's. Dirk found out that little Tommy Eckert's abdominal pain was nothing more than a stomach ache due to eating too many green apples. Everyone at the table laughed when he told about giving Tommy a good dose of Caster Oil. Katherine inquired about the Hentzel baby. David said Martha delivered a healthy baby girl. "Martha was plumb tickled to have a girl after having three boys."

When dinner concluded, David and Dirk checked on Philip. He roused and mentioned that he was in some pain. David gave him some medication to ease his pain.

"Thank you so much for your hospitality, David. With a beautiful nurse like Elizabeth to take care of me, what more do I need?" Philip spoke smiling.

Dirk's jaw tightened as he clenched his teeth shut. He could almost feel the veins pop out in his neck to hear Philip speak about Elizabeth that way.

Changing the subject David asked, "Are you hungry? Katherine made plenty."

"Yes, I am. Is that chicken I smell?"

"Yes, it is," answered David. "I'll have Katherine fix you a plate. I'll get you some fresh water. Is there anything else you need?"

"No, that will be fine thank you."

"Good, I'll be right back," returned David as he and Dirk left the room.

David took Philip in his dinner, including a piece of blackberry pie, while Dirk stole Elizabeth away from the kitchen, escorting her outside.

They walked and talked only a short time when Dirk

mentioned that he had to leave. He was sure to mention that he had enjoyed her company. He thanked her for the invitation to dinner.

Seeing the look of disappointment on Elizabeth's face, Dirk almost told her about his part time job at the iron foundry. He was working a few hours every evening during the week. On Saturday, he put in a half day. It was good pay and he hoped to have enough saved by the end of the summer. He wanted to save up enough to start his own practice. Dirk also wanted to purchase a few household items before asking Beth to marry him. He felt bad that he had to leave so early, but it was nearly time for him to be at the foundry.

Walking towards the house after Dirk left, Elizabeth felt sorry for being so selfish. *He's put in such a long day,* she thought. *He helped unload Philip's things. He made that long trip out to the Eckert's, plus he checked on David's other patients while David was delivering the Hentzel baby. No, doubt he was tired. When he comes Saturday, I'll have a peach pie made just for him.* That was his favorite. Satisfied with her plans, Elizabeth went into the house and up to her room anticipating next Saturday's visit.

Chapter 17

By the end of a few weeks, Philip had started to demand more of Elizabeth's time. He accepted Katherine's help, but requested Elizabeth unless she was busy. Elizabeth found Philip's company to be quite interesting. He told about growing up in Chicago before his family moved to Canton.

One day as she was getting Philip some lunch, Elizabeth thought about how different Philip and Dirk were. She portrayed Dirk rugged and strong, while Philip seemed to possess more refinement. Understanding and to the point described Dirk's speech; Philip spoke with eloquence. Compliments on her attractiveness as well as quoting lines of poetry came from Philip. She didn't even know if Dirk knew poetry. Dirk loves to tease and make her laugh. Philip leans more on the serious side. They seem so opposite, yet she had been attracted to each one in his own way. Dirk had been puzzling lately. The last couple of Saturdays he hadn't come for their usual walks. He said he was busy. She wondered what kept him so busy. Whenever she inquired as to why, he always evaded the question and somehow managed to change the subject. She certainly didn't have time to worry about it now Philip would be expecting his lunch .

Upon Elizabeth's entrance, Philip brightened. "Yellow becomes you," he spoke of her yellow print dress. "You look like an angel with the noon sunshine falling about you."

"Oh, Philip, you always flatter me," said Elizabeth blushing slightly.

"And I always speak the truth. Come," he motioned. "Sit down at the table and practice your typing while I devour this feast you've prepared me."

Philip had David bring his typewriter from town. He had been teaching Elizabeth how to type each afternoon. She sat down and began to practice the drills he had written for her previously.

"You learn so quickly," he complimented.

"Do you really think so? I'm enjoying it immensely," she replied looking up from her work.

"Yes," Philip went on to say. "In a few more weeks you will be typing as fast as the best newspaper reporter."

"I'm not so sure about that," Elizabeth said doubting.

After a few seconds of watching her type, Philip revealed a plan. "Why I have a brilliant idea my dear, Elizabeth." He reached over and put his hand on top of hers causing her fingers to fumble misspelling a word. "When I'm rid of this dreadful cast, I shall be in need of an assistant. You and I would make a great team, Elizabeth."

"Philip, you can't be serious. I know nothing of running a newspaper," she expressed.

"I will teach you all you need to know. It will be splendid," he encouraged with enthusiasm.

"Have you forgotten, Philip, that I assist my brother in his work?" voiced Elizabeth rising to her feet. She put thoughts of working with Philip out of her mind.

"Just listen to me, Elizabeth," he pleaded. "If we were partners, your name would be at the end of every column along side mine in bold print. Your name would be known throughout the entire county. Just think about it is all I ask."

"Is there anything else I can get you before I leave. I need to tend to the girls," spoke Elizabeth changing the subject.

"Can't the girls tend to themselves? Don't get me wrong they are sweet little things, but Elizabeth I need your company. I will go absolutely crazy if I'm cooped up in this room with no one to talk to all day."

"I'm sorry, Philip," she apologized. "But I promised the girls that I would spend the afternoon with them."

"Well, if you must, but I will look forward to our reading of the newspaper this evening. That is if your time hasn't already been committed to something else," spoke Philip in a rather pouting disposition.

"Of course not, Philip. I'll be right in after dinner. If you need anything, Katherine is here."

Elizabeth left the room before he could talk further. She found Kate and Sarah patiently waiting. She felt badly that she had neglected to play with them for the past few weeks. She didn't like having Philip upset with her either, but after all she had promised them.

Kate, Sarah, and their Aunt Elizabeth enjoyed the afternoon together. After swinging and jumping rope, they decided to cool off in the creek. As they waded, Elizabeth chuckled to herself as she reminisced the time Dirk had taken her and the girls on a picnic. They had such a good time that day. *That's odd,* she thought. *I haven't even thought of Dirk the past few days. I guess I've been preoccupied with Philip's convalescence. It doesn't appear that I'm much on Dirk's mind lately,* she reasoned. *I see him only on Sundays. Maybe he doesn't feel for me the way I thought he did. Maybe I'm all wrong about Dirk,* she argued with herself. *I'm not being fair. He has shown every intentions of wanting to marry, he just hasn't asked.* Elizabeth brought herself to the present scolding herself for thinking on such things now. She needed to focus her attention on the girls.

The afternoon passed quickly and they soon headed back home. Elizabeth took the laundry off the line for Katherine before going into the house. David came home later. He took a copy of the newspaper into Philip as he requested every day. Philip eagerly ate up every word, but saved portions for he and Elizabeth to read together.

When dinner dishes were washed and put away, Elizabeth went to Philip's room as usual and wrapped lightly on the door.

"Come in, come in," beckoned Philip.

Opening the door, she walked in. Elizabeth had enjoyed her day so much. She hoped for some time to herself this evening. Maybe she wouldn't stay too long to read.

Philip wasted no time once he knew it was Elizabeth. "My precious flower and rarest gem, I have been beside myself with boredom all day without your presence. Please come sit beside me. Promise me you won't leave me alone tomorrow," he said rather dramatically.

"You weren't alone, Philip. Katherine was here all day," replied Elizabeth.

"Yes, yes I know, but it's your presence that I long to see walk through that door every time it opens," spoke Philip with compassion.

"Well, I'm here now," said Elizabeth. "I see you've finished with your supper. Is there anything else you need before we read the paper?"

Philip sat up as straight as possible and spoke in a serious tone. "There is something I need, Elizabeth."

Elizabeth was taken back by his deep serious attitude. He didn't normally call her just by her given name. She walked over to him and checked his forehead for any sign of fever.

"What is it, Philip? Are you in any pain?" she asked solemnly thinking he may be ill.

Philip took Elizabeth's hand and pulled her down into the straight back chair that sat beside his bed. "Nothing is wrong, Elizabeth. Everything is right can't you see? I need you. Will you marry me, Elizabeth?"

Quickly withdrawing her hand, Elizabeth sat speechless for a few moments before she spoke. "I don't know what to say, Philip. This is quite a surprise." She rose from her chair thinking. She enjoyed talking to Philip, but wasn't sure she was willing to spend a life time with him.

Philip went on speaking. "Since being left alone today, I did some thinking. This is the perfect solution," he blurted out with enthusiasm. "I need a business partner and a wife. You fit both of those categories. Ours will be the perfect marriage. So, my precious pearl, will you do me the honor of becoming my wife?"

Elizabeth took a deep breath then began. "Philip, I'm very flattered that you asked, but I don't love you. When I marry, I want it to be for love." She tried not to be too hard on him. She hoped that he would take it the right way.

He was not to be shaken. Her words seemed to give him inspiration, and he plunged on ahead with more philosophical reasoning. "Oh, Elizabeth, I believe you do love me. You just haven't realized it yet. The way you've taken care of me, you've been my constant companion through sickness already." He hesitated only long enough to catch his breath. "It was wrong of me to ask so abruptly I know. Please forgive me. Just think about what I've said and give me your answer tomorrow. I'll be able to give you anything your heart desires, my cherished one." When he finished, Philip Morgan reclined on his stack of pillows in satisfaction like a lawyer that had just given his concluding comments.

Elizabeth thought for a brief moment then decided on the safest course of action. "Philip, I'll pray about it."

"Do whatever you feel necessary," replied Philip smugly. Then he changed the subject as though the matter was settled. "Now let's begin our reading, shall we?"

"I'm sorry, Philip, I don't feel up to it tonight," she responded starting to leave. "I'm tired. I think I'll turn in early this evening."

"Of course my flowering rose. You go right on to bed. I'm sure you have plenty of wedding plans to ponder," he said smiling broadly with a sense of accomplishment.

"But, Philip, I didn't say I would marry..." protested Elizabeth. She was cut off by Philip.

"Now, now no negativism before bedtime. Good night and pleasant dreams, my queen." He reached for the newspaper, opened it up, and began reading as though Elizabeth had already left the room.

Feeling a bit confused by what had just occurred, Elizabeth called out a meek good night before she left his room.

Relieved to have the evening to herself, she started up the stairs to her room. A knock came from the back door. She couldn't imagine who would be coming at such an hour unless someone desperately needed David. She heard her brother answer the door. He called her name. Elizabeth descended the stairs to find Dirk standing in the doorway.

"Hello, Beth, I thought maybe we could just sit out on the porch for a while," Dirk offered.

They hadn't been together for a few weeks except for church and dinner on Sundays. It seemed like Dirk's business or Philip Morgan always interfered.

The couple stepped onto the porch before Elizabeth spoke. "I'm surprised to see you, Dirk. You've been so busy lately," she said in a snug manner. She was glad to see Dirk, but was a little annoyed at the way he had been avoiding their walks on Saturdays.

Dirk could tell by the tone of her voice that Elizabeth was upset with him. He just couldn't tell her about the extra job, that would ruin the surprise. If he could only keep it from her for a few more weeks; things would be perfect. He responded to her apologetically. "Please don't be sore at me, Beth. I'm here tonight because I wanted to see you."

"So does this mean you won't be coming tomorrow evening again?" she asked curtly. She knew she wasn't being fair, but she was irritated with him and confused with Philip. This was not a good time for him to come. All she wanted was the evening to herself. Selfishness had over taken her, but she didn't care. It just seemed like all her time and energy had been spent on everyone else. It left none for her. Any other time she would have been thrilled for Dirk to have surprised her with a visit but not tonight.

Dirk could tell that Beth wasn't herself. He didn't know what had happened today, but this was the opposite of what he expected. He tried to answer carefully. "I'm sorry, Beth, But I won't be here tomorrow evening. I thought I explained that."

"You told me you couldn't come. You never explained why."

"I told you I've been busy and I can't get away. Honest, Beth."

Elizabeth's frustration continued to mount as she spoke. "And just what have you been busy doing?"

Dirk knew there was no way to avoid her. He didn't want to lose her trust. "I've taken on a part time job in the evenings at the foundry," he stated with reluctance.

Elizabeth softened slightly, "But why? Can't you afford to stay at the boarding house? I'm sure if you would talk to David, he would make room for you in the office."

"No, it's not that," explained Dirk.

"Then what?" Elizabeth questioned.

"I can't tell you, Beth. Please," he pleaded taking hold of her hands, speaking face to face. "You have to trust me, I'll let you know in time."

"And what if I don't want to wait," she fumed.

SHERRI KAY ROMIG

A lump came to his throat. He didn't know exactly what to
say. He hesitated then answered calmly and serenely. "I guess
that's a choice you have to make. I love you, Beth, with all my
heart."

She pulled her hands free and angrily began to speak as the
built up frustration finally surfaced. "You have a funny way of
proving your love. If this is the way it has to be, I'm not sure I
want it." She changed her tone and spoke rather coolly.
"Philip Morgan loves me. He's asked me to marry him." She
knew in her heart she shouldn't have said that. Elizabeth
knew it would hurt Dirk terribly, but right now she was in no
frame of mind to offer an apology.

Dirk was pierced in the heart by Elizabeth's words. But he
would be devastated if she accepted Philip's proposal. He
knew he risked further wrath, but he had to know. Cautiously
he questioned her. "What was your answer?"

Elizabeth breathed deeply and looked away from him. "I
told him I had to pray about it."

"That was a fair answer."

Dirk spoke with such tenderness it was hard for Elizabeth
not to throw herself into his arms and apologize.

"I'll go now so you can do some praying and deciding." He
tipped his hat and added, "Good night, Elizabeth." And with
a heavy heart, he knew he had to do some praying of his own.
He walked over to where the Doc was. Dirk untethered him,
mounted, and slowly rode away.

He hadn't called her Beth. She could not contain the tears
any longer. She ran into the house and straight to her room.
She readied herself for bed in haste. In the darkness of the
night, she prayed and cried herself to sleep.

112

Chapter 18

Elizabeth couldn't believe it; she was going home. She was on the Monday afternoon train. Katherine and the children were going along as well. It had been since Christmas that any of David's family had been to visit the Grafton clan. The girls were excited about going to see their grandparents. Katherine had been the one to suggest the visit. Elizabeth had mixed feelings about leaving, but Katherine had noticed how worn out Elizabeth had become. At first Katherine suggested that Elizabeth make the trip, but David suggested that Katherine and the children visit as well. He mentioned to Katherine that she and Elizabeth needed a break, and she agreed. David told them not to worry about Philip. He had given him some crutches so he could get around and do for himself.

The morning had been full of activity as everyone tried to get ready for the trip. Katherine and the children were to be gone for only a week. David and Katherine informed

Elizabeth that she could stay as long as needed. Sitting in the seat beside Elizabeth was Kate. Sarah and Katherine, who was holding young David, sat facing them.

They had been riding about an hour when one by one the children succumbed to the lull of the train. Katherine was glad, for she knew it would be a long trip for them.

Elizabeth relaxed in her seat. Her mind was whirling with the events that had taken place in the last few days. Elizabeth had unfolded the whole story to Katherine about Philip's proposal and Dirk's departure on Friday evening. She was relieved that Philip had accepted her answer not to marry him. He seemed to take it in stride, for that she was thankful. Deep in her heart, Elizabeth knew Philip was not for her. For one thing, she couldn't call Philip a Christian. He went to church occasionally and appeared to be a good moral person, but Elizabeth knew that was not enough. Dirk was the one to whom she pledged her devotion, yet she had treated him so poorly that night he came for a visit. She had wanted to apologize but never got the opportunity. He usually sat in their pew on Sundays but not yesterday. Elizabeth caught a glimpse of him just before the opening song. He was seated in the back. She hoped to talk to him after the services, but when she made her way to the back he was gone. He didn't even come for Sunday dinner. She felt sick and unable to eat much just thinking of how she had treated him. She wondered what he thought of her.

Tears now started to well up in her eyes. Through blurred vision, she noticed Katherine handing her a handkerchief along with a small, white box.

"Thank you, Katherine," Elizabeth sniffled. "But what's the box for?"

"Open it and see," encouraged Katherine gently.

Elizabeth wiped away the forming tears so she could clearly see the contents of the box. Slowly she lifted the lid and let out a small gasp of surprise. Snugly surrounded by a piece of cotton lay a beautiful, gold, heart-shaped locket. She gently removed the locket from the box and held it in her hands. She opened it up to find an inscription which read, "I love you—Dirk." She closed the locket and clutched it to her heart. Tears flowed freely down her cheeks. She could not hold them back. The locket was from Dirk.

Katherine tried to comfort her the best she could while holding David on her lap.

Elizabeth became confused. She didn't know how Katherine came into possession of the locket. She managed to stop crying so she could carry on a conversation. Besides, she didn't want to awaken Sarah who had fallen asleep across her lap.

Katherine spoke first. "Dirk wanted me to give it to you."

"Why didn't he give it to me himself?" Elizabeth inquired through a few escaping tears.

"He didn't think you wanted to see him," Katherine answered quietly.

"Oh, Katherine, I feel so miserable. I wanted to apologize," spoke Elizabeth with sorrow. "When did he give you the locket?"

"Well," began Katherine, "David went to see him Sunday evening since he didn't come to dinner. When David mentioned that we would be leaving today, Dirk gave it to him. He told David he had wanted to give it to you on Friday evening, but things didn't work out." Katherine concluded by saying, "He loves you very much, Elizabeth."

A fresh stream of tears began to fall as Elizabeth spoke. "I know he does. How could I have been so blind and doubting? He was working all of those extra hours and I accused him of not showing his love and now this." She handed the locket over so Katherine could see. "What am I to do?"

Katherine examined the token of love carefully and commented with a smile, "It's beautiful." Gently Katherine spoke with understanding. "First of all I suggest you put on that locket. Then when you get home, you relax and enjoy some time with your family. And when you're ready to come back, you apologize to Dirk and let him know how you truly feel."

"My first impulse is to get off this train at the next station and go back. If I wait, he may not be there for me," expressed Elizabeth torn in which direction to go.

"Absence makes the heart grow fonder," quoted Katherine. "Dirk will be there you'll see. He's got a good head on his shoulders. He's not about to lose you over one setback that came his way."

"Oh, Katherine, I wish I felt that confident," said Elizabeth drying the last of her tears. She slipped the locket over her head and glanced down with renewed hope in her heart. Looking up at her sister-in-law, whom she thanked God for, Elizabeth said, "Thank you Katherine, for all you've done for me."

"You're welcome," she returned. "I'm just glad I could help in some way."

The train traveled on with Katherine and Elizabeth talking anxiously about seeing family once again. After the children were rested, they wakened up one by one in their own time. They all ate hungrily of the food Katherine had prepared for them. The girls became restless, so Elizabeth read to them from the story book Katherine had brought along.

Nearing late afternoon, Elizabeth became anxious knowing that in a short time she would be home. *Home,* she thought, *it will be so good to see everyone again.* She never realized how much she missed everyone until now. Elizabeth had done some growing up and learned of some valuable lessons in the past few months. The skills she had learned working for her brother were skills she could use no matter where God chose to lead her.

Her thoughts were drawn back to the present as Kate leaned next to her and asked, "Are we almost there?"

Smiling down upon her bright-eyed niece, Elizabeth happily replied, "Yes, Kate, we are."

Elizabeth looked out the window and could see landmarks that were familiar to her. She couldn't help but feel happy. She took Kate's hand and gave it a little squeeze. After a few minutes had passed, the conductor called out that New Lexington was the next stop. Since their trip was on the spur of the moment, there would be no one waiting for them at the station.

Elizabeth couldn't wait to see the look of surprise on her Ma's face. As they stepped off the train, Elizabeth soaked in the sights and sounds of her home town. The places of business and the familiar faces washed over her entire being. This town, these people, her family and friends were the entity that made her who she was.

Each one was glad to stretch their legs as their feet finally came in contact with solid ground. Elizabeth's first impulse had been to go to the livery and rent a wagon and team, but seeing her brother out of the corner of her eye at the lumber mill changed her mind. Observing more closely, she could tell that he was loading a wagon of lumber to be delivered. In her excitement, she almost jumped down off the station platform instead of using the steps. However, Elizabeth did manage to tell Katherine where she was going before she took off in a full run across the street. How unlady-like she must appear, but she didn't care. Her brother was in plain view. As she drew closer, she called out his name. Will turned around in response. He dropped the board he held in his hand, and dashed out in full stride to meet her. Will picked Elizabeth up and swung her around.

"Elizabeth, what a surprise. I didn't know you were coming," spoke Will full of excitement.

"Oh, Will, it's so good to see you too," she replied as she held her brother close. Pulling herself away she continued. "Katherine and I decided to make the trip yesterday. It was spur of the moment. Ma and Pa aren't expecting us."

Will interjected, "Did you say Katherine and the children are here? Are they still at the station?"

"Yes, and I'm sure the girls are getting antsy by now. Is there any way you can give us a ride out to the farm?" she added catching her breath.

"Sure thing," Will returned. "I just need to let Mr. Larmen know. Wait right here and I'll be around with the team." Will soon retrieved the team and wagon and picked up Elizabeth as promised. When they reached the train station, Will embrace his nieces and sister-in-law and held up his little nephew for inspection. "A mighty fine looking boy you have there, Katherine. With those dancing, green eyes, he looks as ornery as my brother," said Will with a chuckle before handing David back to Katherine.

"Thank you, Will," Katherine spoke smiling. "The way I heard it your brother wasn't the only ornery one in the family. Seems to me like I remember a few incidents where you got yourself into a heap of trouble."

"All right, all right," he laughed throwing up his hands in surrender. "I'm guilty. It's good to have you home, Katherine, even though you give me a pretty hard time," he added teasingly as he began loading their bags onto the wagon. One thing he always liked about Katherine was her sense of humor.

After everyone was in the wagon, they started toward the farm. A couple of Elizabeth's friends stopped to talk which delayed them temporarily.

Sarah and Kate were eager to reach the farm. They couldn't wait to run about so they could release some of their pent up energy. Elizabeth had allowed Katherine and little David to sit up front with Will while she rode in back with the girls. Sarah and Kate stood on their knees as they hugged the sideboards eagerly looking. Elizabeth grew more anxious herself with each passing farm. as she clutched the locket in her hand, a smile spread across her face. There was so much to tell her Ma. They had written back and forth, but it was so hard to express everything in a letter. Her mind raced to Dirk. Elizabeth longed to express her gratitude and love for the locket, as well as her apology.

Sarah, being the curious and outspoken girl that she was, noticed the locket that hung from her aunt's neck. She hadn't seen it earlier. *Maybe Uncle Will gave it to her because he missed her so much. Naw,* she reasoned with herself, *he didn't know we were coming.* She could contain her curiosity no longer. She stood up and very carefully stepped over to where her aunt was sitting and nestled in beside her.

"We're just about there, Sarah," spoke Elizabeth.

"Okay," answered Sarah a matter of fact. She reached up to touch the locket. "Where did you get this, Aunt Elizabeth? It's the most beautiful locket I've ever seen."

Elizabeth reached up to caress it with her hand while smiling down at Sarah. "Thank you, Sarah. You're right; it's beautiful. But what makes it even more beautiful and special is the fact that Dirk gave it to me."

"Are you going to marry him?" questioned Sarah looking up to meet her aunt's green, twinkling eyes.

"If he asks me, I suppose I might," grinned Elizabeth trying to tone down the child's imagination.

"I'm going to marry Uncle Will," said Sarah.

"How do you know that?" asked Elizabeth taken back by Sarah's statement.

"Well, I have to finish school first, I know that," spoke Sarah quite grown up. "I love him, and he loves me. Besides, he calls me princess."

"Oh, I see," chuckled Elizabeth within herself.

Elizabeth wasn't about to dishearten her by explaining why that just couldn't be, so she decided to leave the subject alone. She would be sure to tell Will just how much his young niece thought of him.

Sarah, beginning to grow restless asked, "How much farther, Aunt Elizabeth?"

Elizabeth's heart leaped for joy as she noticed how close they were. "Just around the bend, Sarah. Just around the bend."

Chapter 19

Elizabeth awoke to sunshine streaming into her bedroom window along with a pair of cardinals singing a perky melody on a nearby branch outside. She knew she had slept far too late, but she felt rested. Kate and Sarah were still asleep on their makeshift bed of quilts on the floor in Elizabeth's room. The combination of a long trip and staying up later than usual had worn them out she was sure. Elizabeth hoped that Katherine and young David had slept well. Mama had given them David's old room across the hall from Elizabeth.

Yesterday had been quite a surprise to her family, thought Elizabeth as she dressed for the day. She quietly tiptoed around so she wouldn't wake the girls. As she dressed, she reached up and felt the locket. There hadn't been time last night to fill her parents in on Dirk. Pa had given his grandchildren his undivided attention . He took turns swinging the girls around in circles by their arms. Then it was down on the floor, as they each had their turn riding on his back. He tried to buck them off like a wild stallion. They had shrieked with delight and chanted, "More, Grandpa, more." Little David was too young to get involved in the activities, but his grandpa was sure not to leave him out. Seth took David and propped him up on his knees and talked to him for the longest time. Every once and a while David would smile up at his grandpa as if he understood what he was saying. After a short time, his grandpa cradled him in his big, strong arms and rocked him to sleep.

Will had also spent time with each of the children after supper. Elizabeth couldn't help but smile to herself at the attention Sarah showered upon him. She truly had a crush on her Uncle Will. How disappointed Sarah would be when she found out that her uncle was courting Megan Hayworth. No, doubt she would get over it and have a crush on someone else before long. Elizabeth recalled that seemed to be the way with little girls.

Today she, Katherine, and the children would go visit Andrew's family. Emily would be happy to see them. The cousins would enjoy each other's company.

Before Elizabeth reached the bottom of the steps, she heard familiar female chatter coming from the kitchen. She knew Pa would already be out in the fields.

"Good morning," spoke Elizabeth cheerfully.

"Well," replied her Ma with a smile. "I see a good night's rest agreed with you."

"Yes, I slept so soundly. I didn't realize I was that tired."

"Sit down. Elizabeth," insisted Ma. "Let me get you some hot coffee and some breakfast. I've got it warming on the stove."

Ma and Katherine had already eaten and were just enjoying pleasant conversation. Ma put Elizabeth's breakfast on a plate and sat it before her. After saying a silent blessing for her food, Elizabeth began to eat, savoring every bite.

Ma spoke up. "Katherine had been telling me you've all been quite busy the last several weeks."

Not knowing how much Katherine had told her on the subject, she answered cautiously. "Yes, we have."

Just as Elizabeth finished up her eggs, ham, and biscuit, Sarah and Kate came bounding into the kitchen.

"Good morning, Grandma," Sarah anxiously spoke.

"Morning, Grandma," repeated Kate in the same manner as her older sister.

"Well, now," responded Ruth glowing with love for her granddaughters. She gave them each a hug. "Did the two of you sleep well?"

"Yes, ma'am," answered Sarah dramatically. "I'm starved," she concluded by placing her hand on her stomach.

"Me too," agreed Kate, just as emphatically as Sarah had announced.

"Well, spoke Ruth as she looked over to Katherine then back to the girls. "No, grandchild has ever starved while they stayed with me. Elizabeth, will you please get two plates out for these hungry girls?"

"Yes, Ma," responded Elizabeth with a chuckle.

After breakfast dishes were washed and put away, Elizabeth, Katherine, and the children set out to walk over to see Andrew's family. The girls were so excited they ran most of the way.

Before Katherine or Elizabeth made it to the house, they heard shrieks of laughter from inside the house as the cousins greeted one another. Within a few seconds, Emily appeared outside the front door and welcomed Elizabeth and Katherine with open arms.

"Oh, it's so good to see both of you," Emily spoke at once.

"And you," returned Katherine.

"I never realized how much I missed everyone until I came back," added Elizabeth.

"Come on in and tell me news of Dover," beckoned Emily

122

with eagerness. "The children will be just fine playing out by the barn."

So Katherine and Elizabeth followed Emily into the house. They sat down in the sitting room while Emily came from the kitchen and poured them each a cup of lemonade.

The children had a grand time playing together. Matthew at nine years old didn't seem to mind that he was outnumbered by girls. Matthew stood tall and slender with a crop of sandy, brown hair and dark, chocolate eyes. He wore bib overalls and a red shirt that hung out one side of his overalls. Paula's aqua, blue eyes seemed to sparkle in the sunshine. Her midnight hair fell to her shoulder blades with natural curl just like her ma's. She wore a yellow calico dress. Andrew and Emily had two other children. Andrea, who was five and resembled her brother in looks, and two year old Michael, who followed the older children around everywhere.

Since there were quite a few of them, Matthew suggested a game of hide and seek.

"That sounds like fun," agreed Sarah. "We don't play that very often."

"It's settled then. I'll be first," arranged Matthew in a take-charge manner.

"I don't know where to hide," Kate timidly spoke out.

Paula, wanting her younger cousin to enjoy herself while she was visiting, kindly offered to hide with Kate until she got used to the game. Kate relaxed with relief as she took hold of Paula's hand.

Matthew went over to the big, beech tree and leaned his head on his folded arms braced against the tree. "One, two, three…" he began as everyone scattered to find the perfect hiding spot.

Meanwhile, Elizabeth and her sisters-in-law caught up on all the latest news. Emily told them about the newcomers to the area as well as some who had moved further west. She also filled them in on the latest marriages and births. In return,

Katherine and Elizabeth told of their growing town and of the coming newspaper.

"Oh, how wonderful to have your very own newspaper," Emily responded. Then her eyes noticed Elizabeth's locket and she asked innocently, "What a beautiful locket, Elizabeth! Where did you get it?"

With a lump in her throat, Elizabeth glanced at Katherine who smiled with reassurance and answered. "It's from a gentleman friend of hers."

Emily's expression lightened and she beamed with happiness. "Oh, Elizabeth, I didn't know. I'm so happy for you."

Elizabeth ended up pouring out the whole story from how she met Dirk to the last conversation they had together. She even filled Emily in on Philip Morgan.

The trio chatted the morning away, but before they left, Katherine and Elizabeth made sure Emily and Andrew would bring their family over for dinner.

The cousins were disappointed at the thought of ending their fun, looked forward to being together at their grandparents' house later.

The evening supper was a delight. It was always such a wonderful time when all of Elizabeth's family were together. Will had brought Megan to supper. She was a good Christian and ever so sweet. Elizabeth felt a little emptiness for Katherine since David cold not be there. Her own heart tugged downward at the thought of Dirk. Oh, how she wished he could be there to meet her family.

Her thoughts were interrupted as Will stood up at the supper table. "I guess this is the best time to tell everyone," announced Will. He pulled Megan gently to his side. "I want you all to know that I've asked Megan to be my wife."

Seth who didn't miss the opportunity to tease one of his children, responded with quick wit. "What did she say?"

"Oh, shucks, Pa, she said yes," returned Will chuckling. He

realized he should have rephrased his announcement.

Everyone joined in with laughter and congratulations for the happy couple. Megan, who was accustomed to such teasing at the Grafton house, blushed slightly.

"When is the happy occasion to take place?" asked Elizabeth full of curiosity.

"Around Thanksgiving," replied Megan beaming with joy.

"That will give me some time to get the house built before winter. Megan will have time to ready the house with all of those things that womenfolk add to it," he mentioned as he winked at Megan.

After supper the grandchildren didn't hesitate to scurry outside for a game of tag before it got too dark. While the men went into the sitting room to talk of house plans and this year's crops, the women talked excitedly in the kitchen of the coming wedding.

Chapter 20

Thursday afternoon seemed endless as Elizabeth sat on the back steps. Katherine and the children had been gone for two weeks already. It seemed lonely without them. She had decided not to return with them even though she longed to see Dirk. Elizabeth had needed this time of refreshing. The last couple of weeks had been spent helping Emily and Ma finish up the summer canning from the garden. She and Megan also spent time together picking out patterns and material for dresses for the wedding. Megan had asked Elizabeth to be her maid of honor.

Maybe a ride on Belle would do me good, thought Elizabeth growing restless. She had always loved to get on her horse Belle and ride like the wind. She always crossed the pasture and went down through the sloping countryside. She and Will used to race each other when they were younger. It had been so long since she had ridden Belle. She wondered if the horse would even recognize her. Sure enough, Belle nudged Elizabeth just like old times when she harnessed her. Belle was a beautiful, copper, colored mare with white stockings. Within minutes, Elizabeth led her out of the barn.

It was a gorgeous September Day. The trees were beginning to change into their fall apparel. Once outside the barnyard fence, Elizabeth nudged Belle to a full gallop. To feel the breeze on her face and the wind blow through her hair, truly felt gratifying. She went on for a mile or two before turning back. Elizabeth paid more attention to the scenery around her on her way back. This place held so many childhood memories. She chuckled to herself when she came across the big, oak tree that Will had tied her to when they were younger. Will told her that she had been captured. He would come to her rescue. Will had gone to the barn to get something but got distracted and forgot about her. She stood tied to that tree for what seemed like hours until David came along and untied her. Will had felt so bad that he offered her his best knife. Being upset with him, she had refused his knife. He knew he would be in trouble once she told Pa. As she remembered, he had looked so sorrowful that she forgave him and promised she wouldn't tell. She didn't, but David did. Pa made Will clean out the barn stalls for a week all by himself. It was the chore Will disliked the most of all. Thinking of Will, she noticed his wagon leaving the house. *Why would Will come home so early,* Elizabeth pondered, making her way inside the barn. She caught a glimpse of her Ma sitting on the porch. After putting Belle in her stall, Elizabeth gave her a couple of carrots as a treat.

Elizabeth walked over to the house and bounded up the steps with renewed energy and questioned her Ma.

"What was Will doing home?"

Ruth was unsure of what the letter for Elizabeth contained so she very cautiously answered. "Will picked this up at the post office. It was addressed to you so he thought you might want to read it before supper. It's from Katherine."

"That was sweet of him," responded Elizabeth reaching for the letter. "I wonder what Katherine has to say."

Elizabeth carefully tore open the envelope and removed the letter. She couldn't imagine why Katherine would be writing. She and the children had only been gone a few weeks. Her mind raced to Dirk. What if Katherine had written to say he was gone? Beginning to read the penned words, she would know shortly.

Ruth watched her daughter's face change from a state of contentment to one ashen with worry. Meekly she asked, "What does Katherine have to say?"

Elizabeth vaguely hearing her Ma's voice through her tumbling stomach and pounding heart, sat there for a moment motionless. She didn't know if the sound of her voice came out or not. She folded the letter and rested her trembling hands on her lap. Looking up into her Ma's face, Elizabeth felt suddenly drained. She spoke in a soft, listless manner.

"Katherine says Dirk is very sick. He came down with Scarlet Fever a few days ago, and they don't know if he will make it or not."

As soon as the words escaped her mouth, she felt tears beginning to surface.

"Oh, Mama, he just can't die. He just can't."

Ruth moved over to where her daughter sat on the old, wooden, bench. She wrapped her arms around Elizabeth. Even though she had never met this man that her daughter sorrowed after, Ruth could tell Elizabeth loved him. She prayed for the right words to speak, and hoped that she could be of some help. Ruth allowed a few seconds to pass before looking into her daughters pain-filled eyes. She gently spoke with a heart of compassion.

"Go to him, Elizabeth. He needs you." Ruth paused then continued. "Tell him how much you love him, and pray for him."

Choking back the tears, Elizabeth responded, "I will, Ma, I will."

"Saddle up Belle, go into town and purchase your ticket. The fresh air will do you good. When you come back, I'll help you pack for the trip." Ruth knew her daughter would not want to wait until Will or Seth came home with the wagon. Besides, it would help to occupy her time.

Elizabeth was so glad Ma had suggested the ride to town. She always seemed to know just what Elizabeth needed. Elizabeth smiled and gave her Ma's hand a squeeze.

"Thank you, Ma, for being so understanding."

Ruth returned her daughters' smile and nodded, "You're welcome."

They both rose and went into the house in opposite directions. Ruth went into the kitchen to begin supper preparations while Elizabeth fled upstairs to her room to retrieve a small wooden box from her dresser drawer. It contained the money she would need to purchase her ticket.

Elizabeth came down the steps in a flurry. As she reached the bottom, she stopped short to watch her Ma busily working. She should be helping. She began to reconsider making the trip, but suspended the thought when Ruth ushered her out the door.

Elizabeth hastily made her way to the barn. She saddled Belle in record time. As much as she wanted to get to the train station, she didn't push Belle too hard. No, need to hurry she couldn't leave until tomorrow. Tomorrow seemed so far away. She hoped Dirk would still be alive when she got there. She shouldn't entertain such thoughts, but she had to face reality.

"Lord," Elizabeth prayed. "Spare Dirk's life. Give me the opportunity to tell him I'm sorry." She didn't know how else to pray, but shortly after uttering those simple words, calmness took the place of anxiety. Elizabeth knew that only the Lord could give her that assurance. Whatever happened He would be there.

When Elizabeth reached town, she went to the station and purchased her ticket. When she came out, her eyes fell upon the General Store. The thought occurred to her that she should buy Dirk something. Not quite sure what it should be, Elizabeth decided to go have a look.

The bells on the door rang when Elizabeth entered. She had time to browse because Mrs. Foster was helping another customer. Elizabeth looked at everything. Nothing seemed to be what she wanted. Tools seemed too impersonal, yet the beautiful, gold, pocket watch was too expensive. Oh, she didn't know what to do. A book maybe, but which one should she choose? Then her eyes fell on the perfect gift. She would get Dirk a Bible. His had become so worn that the pages were falling out. A smile spread across her face as she thought of him reading the Bible. It was bound in black leather and the words *Holy Bible* were written in gold lettering across the front.

"Is there something I can help you with, Elizabeth?" asked Mrs. Foster cheerfully. "That's a real nice Bible."

"Yes, it is," remarked Elizabeth. "I believe I'll take it."

"Fine, will there be anything else?"

Thinking of her two nieces, she couldn't overlook the jars of candy displayed on the counter. "I'll take two peppermint sticks please."

Elizabeth made her purchases and left the store. She was pleased with the Bible for Dirk. Now, she was ready to return home.

Ma was taking clothes off the line when Elizabeth returned. She couldn't wait to show her the Bible. Elizabeth unsaddled Belle for the second time today, but she didn't mind. Who knew when she would ride her again.

Walking into the yard, Elizabeth pulled out the Bible and handed it to her Ma. She explained that she had bought it for Dirk. Ruth looked it over and agreed that she had made a fine choice. Cheerfully, Elizabeth put the Bible away and the twosome finished their task.

As promised, Ruth helped her daughter pack her bags for the trip back to Dover. Deep inside she knew this would probably be the last time she would spend time alone with Elizabeth.

Will brought Megan for supper that evening. It gave Elizabeth an opportunity to tell her the news of Dirk.

Megan wasn't too keen on the idea of Elizabeth leaving so soon, but she understood completely. "Oh, Elizabeth, I'll miss you. These last few weeks have been like old times. But I know how I would feel if I were you."

"Thanks for understanding, Megan. You are a true friend," stated Elizabeth in earnest.

Megan continued, "If there's anything I can do please let me know."

"Just pray, Megan, pray," Elizabeth pleaded.

Megan gave Elizabeth a hug before answering, "I will."

Before Elizabeth knew it, the evening had ended. Will had taken Megan home. Elizabeth had a hard time falling asleep due to her anxiousness to be with Dirk. She was up early the next morning making her final preparations before leaving.

She chose to wear her burgundy and cream outfit. Her high-collared lace blouse showed slightly beneath her jacket that complimented her skirt. Tucking the last pin into her hair, she placed her hat on top her head and descended the stairs.

It was a rainy day. It would bring cooler weather she was sure. She said her good byes to Ma in the house. There was no sense in everyone riding to the station in the rain. This trip to the station certainly proved to be much different than the first time she left. The first trip was out of duty. She had gone to help her brother. This time a compelling force drew her to the man she loved.

Chapter 21

With the anxiety taking place in the pit of her stomach, she wasn't sure just how much she should eat. When she got to the dining car, she decided on a biscuit, some fruit, and a cup of coffee. She was glad the rain had stopped before she reached Dover. Elizabeth felt her heart begin to beat dramatically. She felt moisture break out in the palms of her hands when the conductor call out that Dover was the next stop. She adjusted her hat, reached for her bag, and stood to her feet when the train came to a stop. Descending the platform steps, Elizabeth felt her legs softening like butter. It was a good thing she told the conductor to send her other bags to David's house, because the walk would do her good.

Approaching the back steps, she took a deep breath and whispered another prayer. She hesitated then wrapped lightly on the door.

It was late in the afternoon so she was not surprised to find

Sarah opening the door. Any earlier and she would have still been in school. Sarah's eyes opened wide with surprise at seeing her aunt. She tumbled out the door and engulfed Elizabeth with a hug. "Oh, Aunt Elizabeth, I'm so glad you've come back. I've missed you."

"I've missed you too, Sarah," replied Elizabeth with joy.

"Sarah, what is going..." began Katherine. At the sight of Elizabeth, she too came outside and embraced her. "I hoped you would come soon."

Still standing outside, the trio gathered their composer and became quiet as if they could read each other's thoughts.

Breaking the silence, Elizabeth asked, "How is Dirk?"

"I won't lie to you, Elizabeth. He's been in and out of consciousness for the past couple of days. His fever remains high. There's not much we can do but keep him comfortable," Katherine spoke in seriousness.

Sarah added, "I'm sure he'll get better now that you're here."

Elizabeth couldn't help but smile after looking into Sarah's hopeful eyes. "May I see him?"

"Certainly," Katherine responded promptly. "Follow me."

The threesome entered the house without another word. At her mother's request, Sarah went into her parents room to entertain her young brother. Katherine led Elizabeth into the spare room where Philip Morgan had spent his time of convalescence. Katherine hesitated at the door. She glanced back at Elizabeth who gave a nod to confirm she was ready.

Katherine walked over to Dirk's bedside and leaned over so he could hear. Gently she spoke, "Dirk, someone came to see you."

He roused and opened his eyes slightly. Katherine stepped back and motioned for Elizabeth to come near.

Before leaving the room, Katherine whispered to Elizabeth. "Since he is so weak, talk only a few minutes."

Elizabeth knelt down at his bedside. With her elbows

resting on his bed, she reached over and gently grasped one of his hands in hers. "Dirk," she quietly beckoned.

Hearing her voice, he weakly opened his eyes, looked into her face, and whispered, "Beth."

Tears started to form in her eyes. Her lips began to quiver. "Oh, Dirk, I came as soon as I heard."

"I told Katherine not to tell you." He closed his eyes and swallowed to gather strength. When he opened them again, his lips formed a slight grin. "I'm glad she didn't listen to me." He took a deep breath then added, "I've missed you."

Her tears gently streamed down her cheeks as she replied, "I've missed you too." Elizabeth hesitated and responded cheerfully, "You're going to get better; I know it."

With his free hand, he tenderly wiped a tear from her cheek. "I will now that you're here. Don't leave me, Beth."

Smiling with encouragement she whispered, "I won't." Not wanting to tire him she added, "You need to rest."

He nodded before closing his eyes.

Lovingly Elizabeth brought his hand up to her lips, kissed it, and whispered, "I'll never leave you again. I promise." She released his hand and quietly exited the room.

Elizabeth sat by his side for two days. He woke only because of thirst. Elizabeth carefully propped his head up to assist him. He burned with fever. Constantly she applied a cool cloth on his forehead. David and Katherine tried to come in and relieve her, but she refused.

On the third night, the longer Elizabeth sat there the more tired she became. She decided to close her eyes for just a few short minutes. She woke to the touch of Dirk's hand resting on hers. It felt cool. She leaned over to check his forehead, and realized his fever had broken.

"Oh, thank the Lord," she whispered. He's going to be all right." She never felt so relieved. She could hardly wait until morning to share the good news with David and Katherine. Sitting there in the chair, she scolded herself for doubting. She hadn't doubted God's ability to heal, but her own lack of faith to trust. It seemed like a lesson she had to repeat over and over again.

Elizabeth passed the next hour until sunrise, reading the Bible by lantern light. She always drew strength by reading the Psalms. Elizabeth read of God's greatness and mighty power. *God is so good,* she thought.

Placing the Bible on the nearby stand, she leaned over to check Dirk's temperature again. Elizabeth found herself studying the masculinity of his facial features. His dark eyelashes, his solid square chin, and his two dimples that appeared whenever he smiled showed so much character.

She was taken by surprise and blushed slightly when he opened his eyes and caught her staring at him. He smiled at her revealing those dimples she had just moments ago imagined being there.

She returned the smile and looked down at him and spoke quietly, "Good morning."

He cupped her face in his hands and drew her close. "I love you, Beth." Dirk ever so softly kissed her forehead. He gazed deep into her sea green eyes and repeated, "I love you."

She answered her love in return. Quickly Elizabeth began to feel remorse for her previous actions. She began to blurt out, "Oh, Dirk, I'm so sorry I ever…"

But he quickly put his finger up to her lips. "Shh, there's no need to talk about that right now. You're here. That's all that matters." He teasingly added, "I would have gotten sick sooner if I would have known you were going to pay me all this attention."

Elizabeth laughed softly and backed away teasingly and shook her head in disapproval. "I'm through being your nurse, Dirk Hampton."

Katherine and David came into the room to the sound of jovial voices. David checked Dirk over and declared, "Well, Dirk, it looks as though the worst is over; you're going to be all right."

Dirk nodded, looked at Elizabeth and winked. "The minute I saw Beth, I knew things were going to be just fine."

"Well, with a week or so to recuperate, I say you should be back to your old self," stated David.

Katherine returned from the kitchen to bring Dirk some broth. She knew he needed something nourishing inside him to regain his strength. After placing the broth beside him, she and David dismissed themselves leaving Elizabeth to care for her patient.

Just as David had said, Dirk gained back his strength and was soon up to taking short walks. Dirk was still under David's orders not to return to work for another week. Dirk felt so useless. He would sure be glad when he regained his strength and energy.

A chilly, October day prompted Elizabeth to insist that her and Dirk go on a picnic. He agreed only after a short resistance, and the fact that she said she had a surprise for him. With her pleading, green eyes, Dirk found Elizabeth hard to resist.

"No, wading in the creek," he teased after they were there.

"I agree with that," she replied. "Let's eat."

Dirk answered heartily, "Sounds good to me. At least I have my appetite back."

They brought an extra blanket for warmth against the chill in the air. After Elizabeth had the luncheon spread out on the blanket, Dirk took the spare and wrapped it around them, like a shawl.

With a twinkle in his eye, Dirk remarked, "Maybe we should always picnic in the cold."

Returning the teasing remarks, Elizabeth replied, "That's enough, Dirk Hampton, or you'll be eating lunch in the cold by yourself."

He just laughed and moved closer to her.

After Dirk said the blessing, they began to eat with little conversation in between. Finishing up with dessert of homemade cookies, Elizabeth broke into conversation. She had never gotten the chance to apologize for her actions from before. It was something she felt she must do.

"Dirk," she began. "I want to apologize for the way I acted before. I never should have talked to you that way or doubted your word. I was just so confused and exasperated that evening you came by. Will you forgive me?"

"I already have, Beth. I should have realized what you must have thought about me taking on another job and not telling you and not coming around. When you told me about Philip Morgan's proposal that night, I didn't know what to say." He looked away from her and admitted, "I went back to the boarding house that night and did a lot of praying of my own."

Taking her hands, Elizabeth turned Dirk's face in her direction. She looked longingly into his eyes. "I never loved Philip Morgan. I love you."

His heart began to pound as he drew her closer. His lips touched hers and she responded in a kiss that melted away any chill of cold that was around them. He distanced himself and took her hands in his. "Beth, I took that extra job at the foundry for us. I wanted the extra money towards lumber for a house of our own and to start my own practice." Hesitating as he knelt on one knee, he nervously asked, "Elizabeth Grafton would you do me the honor of becoming my wife?"

"Oh, Dirk," exclaimed Elizabeth throwing her arms around his neck. "Yes, a thousand times yes. I would be proud to be your wife."

"I wanted to wait and ask you this evening. I wanted everything to be just perfect but now seemed just right."

Elizabeth chuckled as she remembered her Pa's proposal to her Ma. Joyfully she spoke, "This is much better than a chicken coop."

"What?" he questioned with a puzzled look on his face.

"It's just a story of how my Pa proposed to my Ma. I'll have to tell you about it sometime." Changing the subject and pulling her shawl more tightly about her she stated, "It's getting colder."

"Let's head back to the house," Dirk suggested as he began to help with the clean up. "We can tell the good news to David and Katherine."

"Oh, I almost forgot," exclaimed Elizabeth rummaging through the picnic basket. "In all of the excitement, I almost forgot about your surprise." She carefully lifted the box containing the gift out of the basket. With overflowing happiness, she handed the box to Dirk.

He couldn't imagine what it might be. He lifted the lid slowly. There in the box lay the beautiful, black, leather-bound Bible. He removed it from the box and examined it thoroughly. He found an inscription written on the inside cover. It read, "Dirk, to the one I love — Elizabeth."

Looking with admiration at Elizabeth, Dirk closed the Bible. "Thank you it's a perfect gift, and so are you. You've made me the happiest man in the world. God has blessed me more than I deserve." Taking her hand in his, they headed back to the house.

Chapter 22

Stepping out of the boarding house, Dirk started to make his way to the livery to fetch the wagon. It had been good to finally put in a full week of work. Saturday had come and he was on his way to pick up Beth. He found some land to build a house, and he wanted Beth's approval.

He wanted everything to be just right. He took a bath, shaved, and put on a clean, white, shirt with brown pants. He made sure to brush the dust from his Stetson. His heart gave a lurch at the thought of being with his future bride.

Mr. Cole met Dirk at the bottom of the steps. He and his wife, Isabell ran the post office in town. They were a friendly couple.

"Hello, Dirk," spoke Henry Cole excitedly reaching out to shake Dirk's hand.

"Hello there, Mr. Cole, what can I do for you?"

"Oh, no I don't need anything, Dirk," Henry said light heartedly. "We just happened to get this letter on the noon train; it looked important. I thought you might want it right away," finished Henry handing Dirk the letter.

"Why, thank you, Henry," spoke Dirk in gratitude taking the letter.

"You're welcome," replied Henry shoving his hands into his pockets. "I best get back. The Missus will be wondering what happened to me."

"Thanks again, Henry."

"Yep," Henry replied heading back towards the post office.

Dirk took the letter and turned it over. He took in a sharp breath when he saw the red seal and postmark stamped England. How could he, thought Dirk. How did he know where to find me? He was so tempted to open it, but he didn't want to keep Beth waiting. Whatever that envelope contained, could wait. Dirk decided not to let anything ruin his day. He wanted to pick up his bride-to-be and nothing would stop him.

Dirk ran across the street to the livery where Mr. Peterson had the team ready for him.

Filled with anticipation, Dirk pulled up to the Grafton house. He had brought along a blanket for Beth in case she got cold. Nearing the end of October, most of the leaves were off the trees. Sunshine peeked out occasionally from behind the clouds. When the sun shone, warmth could be felt, yet when the sun hid, it became quite chilly.

He jumped down from the wagon like a nervous school boy. He walked up to the door and knocked lightly. Katherine answered and bid him to come in and sit a few minutes. She informed him that Elizabeth was not quite ready.

Eagerly, Sarah visited with Dirk. He put her up on his lap, and asked if she had been a good helper for her Ma.

"Yes, I have," she spoke emphatically. "I gathered the eggs all by myself. Well." she hesitated. "Almost all, Mama had to help me with a few."

"Good for you," remarked Dirk. "It sounds like you were quite a helper today. And how's that little brother of yours?"

"He's fine. He sleeps all night now, but he still doesn't play much."

"You just give him time. I bet come Christmas he'll be sitting up and playing peek-a-boo."

"You think so?" Sarah asked hopefully.

"You can be sure of it," smiled Dirk with a wink.

Hearing the sound of Dirk's voice, Kate awoke from her nap and ran to him. "Want to see my new book?"

"Of course I do," exclaimed Dirk. "What's it about?"

"I'll get it. Be right back," responded Kate scampering off.

Hearing footsteps on the stairs behind him, Dirk turned to find Elizabeth smiling down at him. He put Sarah down, got up to stand, and walked to where Elizabeth stood. Dirk had never seen Elizabeth with her hair down. He was pleasantly surprised at how much more attractive it made her. Her hair fell just below her shoulders. She had the sides brought up into a barrette near the crown of her head. She wore a navy blue skirt and a white blouse. Dirk stared unconsciously until Elizabeth brought him to attention.

"Dirk, is everything all right?" she asked.

"Uh-yes," he said breaking into a smile himself. "Everything is just perfect."

About that time, Kate came running in shouting, "I found my book! You can read it now."

Seeing the look on Dirk's face when Elizabeth came down stairs, Katherine knew his mind would be far from reading a book. Although Dirk would be true to his word, Katherine intervened before he had a chance to reply. "Kate, Dirk and Aunt Elizabeth are ready to go now, but I'm sure he would like very much to read you're book later."

Dirk could see Kate's face suddenly turn long and disappointed. He leaned down, picked her up, and spoke tenderly. "I promise just as soon as we get back I'll read your new book, all right?"

"Promise?" she meekly questioned.

"I promise." And Dirk kissed her forehead before setting her down.

Katherine ushered Elizabeth and Dirk out the door before anymore could be said.

When Dirk and Elizabeth were in the wagon and on their way, Dirk spoke up. "Beth, I just want to tell you how pretty you look with your hair down."

"Are you sure I don't look too much like a school girl?"

"No, you're no school girl. You're a beautiful woman who's going to be my wife. I just wish we could get married sooner."

"I know," she agreed. "But you are the one who doesn't want us to live in the boarding house until the house is built."

"No, Beth, I told you I want to have a house of our own," Dirk reaffirmed. Changing the subject he slowed down the wagon and announced, "Here it is."

"Where?" questioned Elizabeth as she stood in the wagon.

Dirk brought the horses to a stop, then hopped down. He helped Elizabeth down then led her by the hand to the exact location.

"Right here in the clearing," proclaimed Dirk with enthusiasm. "The trees in front will have to be cleared so we have access to the road. And if you look over there," he said standing behind her with his hands on her shoulders directing her. "The creek winds down between those trees. Well, what do you think?"

"Dirk, it's beautiful here. How did you find it? Does anyone own this?"

Dirk beamed with satisfaction. "I thought you would like it here. Actually Mr. Kendle owns the land. Since he's getting up in years, he can't look after it all so he told me he would sell me some."

Elizabeth turned, meeting his gaze excitedly. "When can you start?"

"Well, the way I figure," began Dirk having thought this through. "I'll put in an order at the mill. That should take about a week. The glass for the windows will take much longer. But in the meantime, I'll round me up some help, and get started felling those trees. Our house has a nice sound to it doesn't it?"

"Yes, it does," she nodded. "Oh, Dirk, this is so exciting. I'm going to get started on making curtains and rugs. I'm sure Katherine will help me."

Dirk wrapped one of his arms around her waist and walked her to the wagon. "I just want to get as much done before the ground freezes."

"I'm sure once the lumber is ready, many of the men from the community will be willing to help. We could be in by Christmas," she spoke excitedly.

"Now, who's wanting to get married sooner," he teased helping her up into the wagon. The letter inside his pocket nudged him as he ascended. He answered cautiously. "Let's just take it one day at a time."

"You're right," agreed Elizabeth. "Besides we won't be spending the rest of our lives here anyway. You're still wanting to move out to Colorado to set up your own practice aren't you?"

Sitting beside her in the wagon, Dirk spoke in seriousness. "Yes, I am. I'll be practicing with David for two years. Beth, I want you to be sure you want to do this. You'll be farther from your family, and establishing a practice won't be easy."

Elizabeth looked deeply into the eyes of the man she treasured. She knew God had led her here. And this man who sat next to her was the one whom she wanted to spend the rest of her life with no matter where life may lead them.

She responded with assurance. "I've never been more sure of anything in my life."

That was all Dirk needed to know. Leaning closer he wrapped one arm around her shoulders, while the other hand gently caressed her face. He drew her gently to himself until their lips touched tenderly sealing the commitment that had been pledged between them.

Chapter 23

As promised, when Dirk and Elizabeth returned to the house, he read Kate her book. Katherine graciously bid him to stay for supper. He could not refuse Elizabeth's irresistible smile and the pleading of two young girls.

Dirk and Elizabeth eagerly shared with David and Katherine the news of the land. They told of their house plans that they had discussed.

"It sounds like everything is well underway. I'm sure once the men around here know of your plans, they'll be willing to help," assured David.

"Yes," agreed Katherine. "And if there's anything we can do just let us know."

"Thank you. We will," said Dirk looking at Elizabeth.

Shortly after dessert, Dirk offered his thanks to Katherine for the delicious meal and dismissed himself. Elizabeth walked him outside. The night sky had already begun its cycle.

Elizabeth bid Dirk goodnight from the porch. She waited until he rode out of sight before going inside. She felt like a bird. Her heart soared with happiness. Until now, she hadn't realized it, but the void she had come here with many months ago was now filled. Again God amazed her by his faithfulness.

When Elizabeth went inside, Katherine greeted her with a warm embrace. "I'm so happy for you, Elizabeth. Your wedding probably seems like such a ways away, but time will pass quickly you'll see. Being busy in David's office won't allow much time to set up housekeeping."

"I have some things already. They're in a trunk back home."

"Good," replied Katherine. "Are you taking Dirk back home so he can meet your folks before the wedding?"

"I did want them to meet Dirk, but I just don't know when. He's so busy working with David, and still working at the foundry," Elizabeth answered perplexed.

"What about taking Dirk to Will's wedding at Thanksgiving?" offered Katherine.

"That's a wonderful idea, Katherine. That way I will be able to bring my trunk back with me. I can't wait to tell Dirk tomorrow."

David, Katherine, the children and Elizabeth gathered in the sitting room while David read from the Bible. The girls practiced their Bible verses they had been learning. Before heading off to bed, they had family prayer. Elizabeth had a hard time keeping her mind focused. Her enthusiasm grew when she thought about Dirk meeting her family.

Meanwhile at the boardinghouse, Dirk lit a lamp. He sat down at a small desk in his room. *Today had been good,* he thought. *Beth was happy with the land.* He had enjoyed watching the twinkle of enthusiasm in her eyes that came from her. Everything did seem to be going well as David had said. But Dirk had the feeling that this letter would change all of that. Why did it have to come today? Dirk decided to open the letter and get it over with.

Carefully Dirk broke the seal, and removed the letter from inside. He unfolded it slowly and with a bit of anxiety he proceeded. It read…

My Dearest Grandson,
Although we have never met, you are my grandson.
I am not as young as I once was, and will not be
around on this earth for too many more years.
In the event of my death, you will be the one to
inherit the Hampton Estate here in Asbury. And you
will thus be proclaimed Duke of Asbury. I wish to see
you and discuss matters I am sending you a ticket to
secure your passage here.
Please inform me of your arrival date, so I may have
James, my faithful servant there to meet you.
I trust you will come in haste. There are things about
me you need to know.
Sincerely,
Lord Richard Hampton
Duke of Asbury

Dirk put the letter down in disbelief. He sank back into the chair with his arms crossed in front of him. His mind instantly filled with mixed emotions. His heart beat furiously inside him as he stood up to pace the floor. What right had his grandfather, whom he had never met, demand that he come to England. He wouldn't go he decided. Then his thoughts pondered the words his grandfather had penned. *"There are things about me you need to know."* What did he mean by that?

Dirk sat down once again putting his head in his hands contemplating a decision. His mind turned to Beth. *What is she going to think of me for not telling her that I come from a wealthy heritage. What if she decides not to marry me? Even if she does, will she understand if I just up and leave to find some lost grandfather?*

146

Thoughts plagued Dirk's mind for what seemed like hours. He knew this was something that needed God's direction. *If only I would have known what this letter contained earlier, I would have asked David for advice.*

After praying earnestly for some time, Dirk decided to visit Pastor Thompson. He knew that he often stayed up late preparing for his Sunday sermons. Maybe he would still be up. The only other obstacle was Mrs. Flanagan. Dirk knew her rule, but silently prayed as he descended the steps that she would have a change of heart.

Dirk found her finishing up the last of the supper dishes. Part of his prayers had been answered. When he told her he wanted to speak with the pastor, she graciously gave Dirk a key. Mrs. Flanagan asked only that he return the key in the morning at breakfast.

Pastor Thompson's house sat near the church on the way out of town. Dirk figured a brisk walk in the cold night air would help. Upon reaching the pastor's house, he noticed a light in the kitchen. Dirk knocked lightly on the door.

Pastor Thompson greeted him warmly. "Dirk, come in. What a pleasant surprise. You must have something important on your mind to come at this hour."

"Yes, I do. I hope you don't mind me interrupting your studies," spoke Dirk apologetically.

"Not at all. I was just about finished anyway." Pastor Thompson led him into the kitchen where he offered Dirk a chair and a cup of coffee.

Dirk had always found the pastor easy to talk to and tonight was no exception. Dirk told the pastor of all the events that had taken place in the last twenty four hours.

Attentively the pastor listened to everything Dirk said.

"I just don't know what I should do," summed up Dirk in exasperation. He took a sip of coffee, relaxed back into the chair and waited for a response.

Pastor Thompson sat silent for a few moments before

offering his council. After weighing all of the options, the pastor summarized his thoughts.

"Well, Dirk, he is your grandfather and he has a soul. His time is limited upon this earth. Maybe the Lord is giving you this opportunity to witness to your grandfather about the Lord before he dies. And as far as Elizabeth is concerned, if she truly loves you she'll want what's best for you. The Bible talks about love. In I Corinthians the thirteenth chapter, it says love is not selfish. I'm not saying that Elizabeth will be thrilled with the idea of your leaving if that is what you decide. I'm just saying that I think she will understand. But the ultimate choice is yours. Let's pray. We'll ask God to grant you direction and peace in whatever your decision may be.

Dirk agreed and they both bowed on their knees right there in the kitchen seeking God's help. When they were finished, Pastor Thompson gave Dirk a big, old, bear hug. The pastor told Dirk that he would continue to pray for him.

Dirk thanked him and took his leave. Even though his heart and mind were still heavy, he knew God would answer.

After entering his room, he prayed once more before going to bed, When Dirk did settle into bed, the pastor's words kept replaying over and over in his mind. His grandfather had a soul.

Chapter 24

Dawn came sooner than Dirk had anticipated. A lack of rest the night before left Dirk awfully tired. He got up and readied himself for church. After praying once more, a sense of peace and assurance guided him to what he should do. Dirk descended the stairs and entered the dining area where Mrs. Flanagan was serving breakfast. He returned the key and sat down to eat breakfast with the other boarders. Dirk settled on a cup of coffee. None of the aromas from Mrs. Flanagan's fine breakfast tempted his appetite. The other boarders tried to make conversation, but Dirk didn't feel much like socializing. Occupied with his decision, he finished his coffee and headed over to the livery to fetch the wagon and team. Dirk decided to drive out to the Grafton's. He would be earlier than usual, but he hoped Beth would be ready.

When he pulled up, David had just finished hitching up his own team. "Good morning, Dirk."

"Morning," Dirk replied. "Is Beth ready?"

"I believe so. She and Katherine were fixing the girls' hair. Come on in and have a cup of coffee before we leave for church," David volunteered leading the way into the house.

Dirk stepped inside just as Elizabeth finished tying a ribbon in Sara's hair. Seeing Dirk, her eyes lit up. She walked over to where he stood by the door.

"Come on in and sit down. "I'm glad you're early. I want to talk to you about something," said Elizabeth bubbling over in excitement.

"No, I-um," Dirk stammered and hastily changed the subject. "Are you ready to go? I thought maybe we could leave early. I have something to tell you too."

"Yes, I'm ready," she spoke hesitantly. "Are you all right? You sure you don't want to sit down?"

"I'm fine, he said smiling. "You look pretty today."

Elizabeth blushed slightly and responded with a thank you before quickly grabbing her coat from off the hook.

Dirk and Elizabeth walked outside without another word. Elizabeth thought Dirk was behaving a little strangely, but she decided not to question him. She refrained from blurting out the idea of meeting her folks. Elizabeth thought for a moment. *He did say he wanted to tell me something. Maybe Mr. Peterson has changed his mind about selling the land.* She decided to remain silent, and let Dirk speak his mind.

They rode in silence for a short distance. Slowly Dirk brought the horses to a halt. The sun was out. Beth would not get chilled while they talked.

Dirk gave Elizabeth a weak grin before breaking the silence. "I'm sorry, I haven't been too talkative this morning. You mentioned that you had something to tell me. Do you want to go first?"

Elizabeth hesitated, and thought whatever he had to say must be more important. She decided to let him speak first. Afterward she would cheer him up with her good news.

150

"No, Dirk, you go first."

He didn't argue. He cleared his throat and asked Beth to hand him his Bible. When she gave it to him, he removed the letter from its envelope and handed it to her.

"Here," he said with gentleness. "I want you to read this."

Elizabeth took the letter and began reading. She felt her heart drop to the pit of her stomach. A hundred thoughts and questions raced through her mind. When she finished, she laid the letter on her lap and stared blankly out in front of her for a few moments. She felt somewhat betrayed and confused.

Finally she commented while looking directly at Dirk in seriousness. "I don't quite understand. What are trying to tell me? Are you from royal descent?"

Dirk was not sure how to begin. "Yes, and no."

He noticed Beth beginning to squirm a little on the seat, but he went on to explain.

"You see my grandfather is Lord Richard Hampton. He owns a very large estate. When my father was growing up, marriages were arranged between families of wealth. But, when my father became of age to marry, he had fallen in love with someone else."

"Your mother?" questioned Elizabeth in sincerity.

"Yes, my mother. And unfortunately for my father's sake her parents weren't among the socially elite. My mother's parents had been good friends of my grandparents. They even frequented each others estates, but they weren't financially equal."

"You mean he couldn't marry her just because her parents didn't have as much money as your grandparents?" Elizabeth questioned in disbelief.

"Yes, and they had already chosen someone else for him. When he tried to explain to his parents that he loved Margaret, they told him that was just not how things were done. They tried to convince him that in time he would love Gwendoline just as much."

"Well, what did your father say to that?"

"There wasn't anything to say. His future had been already planned. He went along with the wedding preparations. A few weeks before the wedding, he and my mother secured passage on a ship and came to America. They asked the chaplain on board to marry them."

"How did your grandparents find out?"

"He left them a letter denouncing any title or inheritance that belonged to him. My father wrote them saying, that he would not marry if it wasn't for love. In the letter he informed them of his plans to sail to America. My grandparents were outraged."

"And what about your mother's parents?"

"They were only sorry that their daughter had to be so far away. They were happy for them. My father wrote to his parents when he and my mother settled in America. My grandfather wrote a return letter stating that he had dishonored the family name and his actions were unforgivable. Grandfather said my father would never inherit the Hampton Estate. After a period of time, my grandmother wrote to my father. She told him that she forgave him. She sought his forgiveness as well. She said she should have been more understanding. She gave him and my mother her blessing. They kept in touch for many years."

"Did your grandfather ever forgive him?" Elizabeth asked in concern.

"As far as I know, he never did," sighed Dirk looking away.

Elizabeth spoke. "After all of these years your grandfather wants you to come to England?"

Dirk looked deep into Elizabeth's eyes and said, "Yes, and that's why I never mentioned my grandparents to you. I haven't heard from them until now."

Elizabeth's heart went out to this man she loved. She instantly had a greater love and appreciation for Dirk's parents, whom she had never met. Their sacrifice and love for each other proved amazing.

Reaching over, she took Dirk's hand and advised softly.

"You need to go to him. He needs you."

Dirk couldn't believe what he was hearing. She actually thought he should go. "Are you sure? It's just not a days trip on the train you know. I'll be gone for at least a month. The house won't get started before the ground freezes. We'll have to wait until spring. We won't be able to get married when we planned," he explained all in one breath.

Very calmly and meekly Elizabeth replied with assurance, "I'm sure."

Dirk took her in his arms, held her close, and whispered in her hair. "You don't know how much that means to hear you say that, Beth. I'm going to miss you."

"I'm going to miss you too," she returned holding tightly to his waist with her face buried in his chest.

Elizabeth conjured up the nerve to ask, "How soon will you be leaving?"

"I'm not for sure. Maybe by the end of the week. Oh, Beth, I wish I could take you with me, but I don't even know how things will be when I get there."

"I know. I'll be fine, really. I'll pray for you every day," she added trying to sound encouraging even though her heart was breaking on the inside.

Feeling much relief, Dirk responded, "I'll wire the minute I get there." Sitting up straight and taking the reins back into his hands, he suddenly remembered that Beth had something to say. "You mentioned you had something to tell me. What is it?"

Elizabeth knew that the news she had was not important now, so she tried to dismiss the thought.

"Oh, it's nothing. It doesn't matter now."

"Yes, it does matter," insisted Dirk. "Now out with it."

Elizabeth fiddled with the pleats in her skirt as she talked. "I had wanted you to make the trip with me to attend my brother's wedding so you could meet my parents."

Dirk swallowed hard recognizing the disappointment in

her voice. "Beth, I'm sorry. Look, I can forget about this whole thing. I'll go with you. I won't leave until after Thanksgiving." She interrupted with a half smile. "No, you need to go now. Besides the sooner you leave the sooner you'll return."

"If that's what you want," he questioned uneasily.

Elizabeth nodded then threw herself into his arms. She wanted to cry so badly, but she knew she mustn't or Dirk would be sure to change his mind. So she just clung to him taking in the smell of his shaving lather, the fresh scent of his shirt, and the steady rhythm of his heart.

Dirk instinctively returned her embrace and whispered, "I love you."

After a few moments, Elizabeth took a deep breath and slowly pushed away. She had a determination to make the most of their time together. She flashed Dirk a bright smile and settled back in the seat and announced, "Well, we'd better get going or we'll be late for church."

Dirk swelled in side with a greater love for this woman sitting by his side. He picked up the reigns and urged the horses onward.

Chapter 25

Friday had come with much activity. Elizabeth had been writing in David's files which patients had received what medications along with the amounts. David and Dirk were in the back discussing a new medical procedure. Roy Spencer, a gangly, red headed, eleven year old came tumbling in the door, and handed Elizabeth a copy of the day's newspaper.

"I'm sorry, Roy," explained Elizabeth. "But I didn't send for the paper."

Roy returned with plenty of enthusiasm. "I know, Miss Elizabeth, but Mr. Morgan wanted you to have a complimentary copy today."

"What for?" questioned Elizabeth somewhat confused.

"Just read the front page. It's all about Mr. Hampton," he answered handing Elizabeth the paper. "I better get going. I gotta sell all these papers."

"Thank you," replied Elizabeth unsure as Roy headed out the door.

Elizabeth unfolded the newspaper only to be startled by the heading on the front page. In bold letters it read: "Royalty Living Among Us Commoners." Shocked, Elizabeth read how Philip Morgan had portrayed Dirk. He put him on a pedestal claiming that everyone should bow when in his presence. Philip went on to say that Dirk was going back to England to reclaim his throne.

Before she finished the article, Dirk and David came from the back room inquiring what all the commotion had been about. Elizabeth said nothing. With a sinking feeling, she handed the paper to Dirk.

David stood by Dirk while they read silently. David finished in disbelief that Philip would write such nonsense. Dirk was outraged.

Dirk threw the paper down on the desk in front of Elizabeth. In anger he turned to look at David and Elizabeth. "I'm going over there and take Morgan's typewriter and break it over his head."

Elizabeth stood up impulsively and grabbed his arm. "You can't be serious, Dirk. Just calm down and think rationally."

Dirk spewed back a reply. "That snake in the grass had no right to interfere in my personal business and exploit it to the whole community. He needs to be put in his place."

David who had said nothing so far, agreed. "Dirk's right. Philip Morgan's the type of person who gives journalism a bad name. Something needs to be done."

Dirk was glad David felt the same way. "Thanks, David, that's just what I aim to do. I'm going to put Philip Morgan in his place."

Elizabeth pleaded, "Dirk, just don't do or say anything you'll regret."

"I won't," he agreed as he reached for the door.

Mr. Phelps came in as Dirk opened the door. Fear claimed his countenance.

"What's wrong, Homer?" Dirk asked, temporarily forgetting his own problems.

Mr. Phelps explained about his oldest son, Pete. His boy had been complaining about his side aching off and on for a couple of days. "Today it's worse," explained Homer. "The pain has gotten so bad that at times Pete is doubled over."

David and Dirk looked from Mr. Phelps to each other in agreement. They assured him they would both be right out to the farm.

"Much obliged," Mr. Phelps replied tipping his hat. "I'll let Pete and the Missus know that you're coming." Mr. Phelps left with as much haste as he had come.

"Philip Morgan will have to wait," muttered Dirk grabbing his medical bag.

Elizabeth had a good mind to speak with Philip herself, but she knew this was something between Dirk and Philip. She was curious as to how Philip obtained his information about Dirk. The majority of it wasn't even true. Her thoughts quickly went to Dirk. She couldn't help but chuckle out loud at the thought of him barging over to break Philip's typewriter. She knew Dirk wouldn't actually do such a thing.

Dirk and David reached the Phelp's farm just as Pete experienced another attack. David checked him over thoroughly. He informed Dirk that he had seen a case like this in Chicago.

Dirk remembered studying about appendicitis, but had never known anyone to have the operation.

Carefully David explained the procedure to Pete and his folks. He then asked for consent to operate. After seeing their son in such severe pain, they readily agreed. Dirk and David took Pete back to the office with them. There they had a sanitary operating table, medical tools, and sufficient light.

Upon reaching the office, they found Elizabeth sewing stitches into Mrs. O'Conner's hand. She had been cleaning the lamps in the general store when one of them shattered, cutting her hand. She had requested that the famous doctor take care of her. Mrs. O'Conner was quite disappointed when Elizabeth explained that Dirk was not available. She had been hesitant at first to let Elizabeth tend to her knowing that she wasn't a real doctor. Elizabeth reassured her that she had helped Dirk and David with plenty of stitches. Through the course of the conversation, Elizabeth found out that Mrs. O'Conner told Philip about Dirk. She had been in the post office when the letter arrived and saw the post mark and the magnificent seal. She said she just put two and two together and figured it out.

"I became so excited. I thought everyone should know that we have royalty living among us. It was my idea to put it in the paper. Didn't Mr. Morgan do a wonderful job?"

Elizabeth could tell that she was proud of her accomplishments, and tried to confront her about it not being her business. Mrs. Conner simply argued that a person shouldn't be so secretive about such things.

Elizabeth sewed the last stitch as her brother, Dirk and Pete entered the office. David helped Pete back to the other room. Dirk stopped to see how Elizabeth was getting along. "Well, Mrs. O'Conner," he commented. "I couldn't have done better myself. It will heal nicely. Now if you'll excuse me, I have something else to attend to." Turning his attention to Elizabeth he stated, "Good job, Beth."

Being so flattered and honored that Dirk spoke to her, Mrs. O'Conner asked, "Do you have a royal title or something? How may I address you?"

Being annoyed with the question, he only answered, "Dirk's fine, Mrs. O'Conner." He abruptly turned and went to the back to assist David.

Elizabeth hid her smile.

"He's so modest," bubbled Mrs. O'Conner.

Discreetly Elizabeth ushered her out the door. Mrs. O'Conner was curious about Pete Phelps. She asked Elizabeth many questions about him. Elizabeth simply informed her that their patients prognosis and treatment remained strictly confidential.

After a raise of her eyebrow, a swish of her skirt, Mrs. O'Conner disappointedly took her leave.

The operation was successful. Dirk headed out to tell the Phelps the good news. Coming back into town, he decided to have that talk with Philip Morgan. Although he had cooled off concerning things Philip had printed, Dirk hadn't changed his mind about setting him straight.

As Dirk got off his horse and tied him to the post, he contemplated what he might say. When he stepped into the office of the *Dover Chronicle,* Philip put on a cheesy grin. Dirk changed his mind about the calm approach.

"Where did you get your information, Morgan?" Dirk asked sternly with his jaws set firm.

"Oh, I see you read the article. Is something wrong?" asked Philip evasively.

Dirk repeated, "Where did you get your information?"

"My sources are confidential," spoke Philip coolly.

"Well, your sources are wrong, and you had no right to print something that's not true."

"Oh, come now, Dirk. The towns people want to read exciting news. How intriguing would it have been if I had just mentioned that you received a royal letter?"

"It wasn't a royal letter. What you wrote was a lie. I expect a retraction in tomorrow's paper."

"I'm not sure that can be arranged," Philip stated matter of fact. "You see I've already written the articles for tomorrow's paper. The type is being set as we speak. So I fear there is no room."

Dirk became perturbed. He stepped toward Philip, snatched his pencil from behind his ear and snapped it in two. "Make room, Morgan." Dirk threw the broken pencil on Philip's desk and headed toward the door. Before leaving he turned around and spoke, "You owe Beth a thank you. She told me not to do anything I would regret."

Chapter 26

The end of the week came too quickly for Dirk. He decided to leave on the Monday morning train. That way he could spend one last weekend with Beth and attend church services on Sunday. Dirk had also chose not to work at the foundry Saturday. In fact he had already told Mr. Jenson that he wouldn't be working the later part of the week. Many things needed taken care of before Dirk left. Any mail that he might receive, Dirk had forwarded to David until he returned. He sent word to his mother telling her of his plans. She returned by wishing Dirk a safe journey and offering her prayers. She also sent her love to David's family. Dirk spoke to Mrs. Flanagan earlier in the week. He let her know that she could rent out his room, but she wouldn't hear of such nonsense. She informed Dirk that his room would be kept just like it is. He was grateful and made sure he told her so.

Dirk had contemplated the trip often since his decision. He

had come so close to changing his mind. It would be close to a month before he would see this town, his patients, whom he had become close to, David, Katherine, the children, and of course Beth. He would miss her the most.

Dirk had wanted to do something special with her today. The warm weather for a leisurely ride, picnic, or long walk down the road had past. So he decided to treat Beth to lunch at the restaurant in town. Before he picked her up, there was something in O'Conner's he wanted to buy.

It didn't take long for Dirk to make his purchase. He had been keeping his eye on the gold pin for several weeks. At first, he thought of giving it to her for Christmas, but decided now was a better time. He was glad Mrs. O'Conner had not made any more royal fuss over him. The retraction that Philip printed had quieted wagging tongues.

Temporarily forgetting his departure on Monday, he walked out of the mercantile with a smile on his face. He climbed into the carriage and headed toward the Grafton's

When he walked in, the girls greeted him enthusiastically.

"Close your eyes, girls. I have a surprise for you," compelled Dirk.

"Oh, goody," responded Sarah.

"Yeah!" shouted Kate with glee.

The girls readily obeyed knowing that whatever Dirk had for them would be good. From his coat pocket, he pulled out two peppermint sticks and a few gum drops. He held them out in front of them.

"Open your eyes now."

Kate and Sarah's face lit up at the sight of the yummy surprise that awaited them.

"Candy!" They exclaimed in unison taking possession of the sweet confection.

"Thank you, Uncle Dirk," Sarah announced before taking a lick.

Kate in her excitement took a lick before realizing she had

forgotten her manners. In meekness she quietly expressed a thank you.

Katherine who had witnessed the whole affair teasingly added, "I know who is to blame when their teeth are rotten before they reach adulthood."

Elizabeth joined in the fun. "Did you bring me a peppermint stick?"

"I'm sorry," Dirk added. "I forgot about you."

This brought everyone to laughter.

Katherine bid Elizabeth and Dirk to sit down, but Dirk kindly refused saying he was taking Beth out for the afternoon. Dirk took Elizabeth's coat off the hook and helped her into it. Katherine told them to have a good time before closing the door.

Elizabeth loved surprises and she knew Dirk had today planned. She couldn't wait until they were outside so she could question him.

When they were seated in the carriage, her curiosity could take no more. "What are we going to do today?"

Now Dirk was not the kind to just spill all of his plans, so he decided to tease just a bit.

"Well," he began in a serious manner. "I just thought we might go visit all of our patients one last time."

Elizabeth felt somewhat disappointed until she remembered him doing that yesterday. When she questioned him about it, a smile spread across his face and she knew he was teasing.

"Come on, Dirk," she pleaded. "Just tell me."

"It's a surprise," he responded calmly enjoying every minute of her anxiousness.

She tried to reason, "Can't you give me just one hint?"

"Okay," he agreed as if he was going to surrender. "In what direction are we headed?"

"We're heading toward town," Elizabeth stated, thinking she had him beat at his own game.

Grinning he urged the horses to a trot. "That's right."

Elizabeth waited a few seconds for further explanation. But when Dirk said no more, she spoke up. "Well, what about town?

"I said you were right. We're heading in the direction of town."

"That's it? That's all you're going to tell me?"

"Beth, you said you wanted one hint," Dirk answered mischievously.

Elizabeth rolled her eyes as she spoke, "Oh, Dirk, you're impossible."

"I'll take that as a compliment," he chuckled.

Elizabeth knew it was a losing battle, so she decided to leave it alone and talk of something else. There were so many things she wanted to say and discuss with him before he left. And today was the best opportunity. She had him all to herself most of the day. Later this evening, David and Katherine had invited him to one last dinner. Tomorrow after church, she and Dirk had been invited to Pastor Thompson's house.

Elizabeth was pleasantly surprised when they pulled up to the town restaurant. She had eaten there on one or two occasions. The Campbell's served a delicious menu of food.

Seeing them walk in, Mrs. Campbell seated them at a table for two in the most remote corner of the restaurant. Dirk thanked her and she left them.

Doreen Campbell was an attractive woman in her late forties. She and her husband, Hollis had never been able to have children. Elizabeth had felt sorry for them. Doreen always seemed cheerful. Elizabeth had often observed her around children. There seemed to be that longing in her eyes for one of her own.

A blue-checked table cloth covered their table. Two menus were face down at each place setting. Mrs. Campbell gave each one a glass of water. She would return to take their order. During their time in the restaurant, Dirk and Elizabeth talked, laughed, and enjoyed one another's company.

After eating, Dirk drove to the land that would someday be the site of their home. Dirk grabbed Elizabeth by the waist and swung her down from the carriage. They walked hand in hand to the vicinity of where their house would stand. Releasing Elizabeth's hand, Dirk reached into his coat pocket and removed a small box. He handed it to Elizabeth.

"What's this?" she questioned.

"Open it and see. I was going to save it for Christmas, but I want to give it to you now."

Elizabeth opened the box carefully. She took in a sharp breath. Inside was the gold watch pin. It was round with a filigree bow attached to the top. The face of the watch was white with black numerals and hands.

"It's beautiful, Dirk, thank you," she said with a small tremble in her voice. Elizabeth thought she might cry.

"I'm glad you like it," expressed Dirk.

Elizabeth removed the pin from it's box and pinned it securely to her blouse. "I'll wear it everyday."

"Oh, Beth, I'm going to miss you," replied Dirk with a troubled heart.

Elizabeth wiped away a few escaping tears. The couple stood facing each other appearing silent. But the language of love they communicated through their eyes was more than words could express.

Chapter 27

Sunday service slipped by quickly. Dirk wanted to savor every portion. He didn't know when he would be back. Dirk hoped he could find a little country church such as this in England. He had heard of many fine and fancy churches there. Aside from the great architecture, he hoped to find one that just preached the simple truth of the gospel. Pastor Thompson's message had been a fine example of that this morning. It had been just what Dirk needed. He thought perhaps the Pastor had preached with him in mind. Pastor Thompson had preached of experiencing joy and peace in your heart when you are in the will of God. Surely Dirk had experienced that when he surrendered to God his relationship with Beth and the trip to England.

Many people approached Dirk after service wishing him a safe journey and offering their prayers.

The majority of Sunday afternoon for Dirk and Elizabeth

was spent with the Thompson's. They were such good people. Not only was he an interesting preacher, but he and his wife Charlotte were friendly, practical, and hospitable. The Thompson's have five children of their own. All of whom are grown, and most have families of their own.

When they arrived, the Pastor took Dirk into the sitting room while Elizabeth helped Charlotte in the kitchen.

They sat down to a fine meal. Pastor Thompson asked Dirk if he would offer the blessing. During the meal, an array of conversation topics swirled around the table.

After eating, the Thompson's graciously ushered Dirk and Elizabeth into the sitting room. Elizabeth offered to help Charlotte with the dishes, but she quickly refused.

"I'm just going to rinse them off. Those dishes aren't going anywhere," explained Charlotte. "I never like to fuss with dishes when there's company to enjoy."

Elizabeth decided to tuck that piece of advice away in her memory for when she and Dirk would entertain company. The more Elizabeth got to know Charlotte Thompson, the more she was drawn to her. Her love and hospitality radiated through everything she did or said. It was a quality that Elizabeth decided she needed to work on in her own life.

In the sitting room, the pastor steered the conversation into a more serious setting.

"So, Dirk, how long will you be staying in England?"

Dirk sat up and leaned forward. He clasped his hands in front of him while resting his forearms on his legs. "I'm not for sure. To sail will take about ten days, if the weather's good." He glanced back at Elizabeth who was seated beside him. "How long I stay depends on my grandfather. I only want to stay long enough to find out what he wants with me. Besides, this is the man who cut off my father from his family."

"Are you angry with him?" questioned the pastor.

Dirk thought for a few moments before answering. "I was at first, but I've forgiven him. I guess I'll stay as long as it takes to sort things out. I just don't want to be gone from Beth too long."

Pastor Thompson chuckled, "I can understand that."

Mrs. Thompson dismissed herself, but returned in a short time beckoning everyone back into the kitchen where she served cake and coffee.

Not wanting to wear out their welcome, Dirk and Elizabeth spoke of leaving. They did not do so without another invitation to come back from the pastor and his wife when Dirk returned. They gladly accepted.

Dirk and Elizabeth had enjoyed their visit immensely. They had a real opportunity to get to know their pastor and his wife better. They found them to be genuine and sincere people.

When they reached the Grafton house, Sarah and Kate announced their arrival. The girls presented Dirk with pictures they had drawn. Elizabeth could tell that he was deeply touched by their thoughtfulness. To prove his appreciation, he read a few of their favorite stories. When story time ended, David and Dirk started out to play a simple game of checkers. The best two out of three turned into the best five out of six. Each time a game ended, the loser vowed to win the next one. From Katherine and Elizabeth came laughter as each game ended. But only a look of serious competition arose between the men. The games ended in good humor and a handshake. The aroma of corn popping over the fireplace infiltrated the whole house. Everyone was having a grand time.

Shortly before Dirk took his leave, Katherine put the girls to bed. She and David talked quietly in the kitchen leaving Dirk and Elizabeth some time to themselves in the sitting room.

Elizabeth presented Dirk with the gifts she had intended to give him for Christmas. She had made Dirk a dark, green, plaid shirt. Elizabeth had also knitted him a brown, woolen, scarf. She stayed up late last night to finish.

Smiling broadly, Dirk wrapped the scarf around his neck. He held the shirt up for observation. "You do fine work, Beth. The shirt will fit perfectly. The green will remind me of your eyes," he mentioned with a wink. I'll be needing a scarf with the colder weather coming. Thank you. I will wear it often, and in a way it will keep me close to you." He took a deep breath into the scarf. "Lilacs, I hope the scent of you stays on this for as long as I'm away."

It was getting late, and Dirk needed to be leaving. Thanking Elizabeth once more for the fine shirt and scarf, Dirk headed for the door where he put on his coat. Once outside the door, he seemed to jump into the rig. *Tonight had been fun,* he thought. The Grafton's had become so much a part of him. They were like his own family. Dirk experienced a deep ache inside himself as he drove away. He wanted so much to turn the team around and stay. It had been so hard to leave her. The scent of lilacs urged him onward.

Chapter 28

Taking one more look around his room in the boarding house, Dirk closed the door. In one hand he carried a traveling bag, and in the other a small trunk. He had said good bye to Mrs. Flanagan last evening before going to bed. However he decided to have a cup of coffee before leaving for the station. In the dinning room, sat a parcel of food that Mrs. Flanagan had kindly made him. Dirk didn't take the time to sit down. He graciously thanked her, drank the coffee, and departed.

The brisk, cool air greeted him as he stepped outside. Looking up into the gray, massive, clouds Dirk could tell the hint of snow was in the air.

The walk to the station seemed to be the longest he had ever taken. He placed the small trunk on the platform and stepped inside. The station seemed rather calm. As far as he could tell, there would be only a few others besides himself that would be boarding the train. Just as he was about to sit down, David came through the door. He was followed by the rest of his family including Elizabeth.

Elizabeth wore a navy blue dress with a white, lace collar. She had worn her hair down just for him. Dirk stood mesmerized by Elizabeth, which caused him to stare. The lighting in the station softened her appearance, making her appear like a dream. Dirk reached out to be sure, but his dream ended when Kate and Sarah ran into him throwing their arms around him. Elizabeth laughed at the sight and Dirk joined in.

Katherine and Elizabeth had also prepared Dirk a sufficient lunch and supper. He thanked them and managed to put it into his bag along with Mrs. Flanagan's supply. He wouldn't go hungry that's for sure.

Dirk pulled out a peppermint stick and gave it to each of the girls. Quite alert and observant to everything around him, young David sat in his mother's arms. When Dirk grasped his fingers and spoke to him, he smiled.

The sound of the train's whistle could be heard in the distance. David looked down at his watch and remarked, "It looks like you'll be leaving right on schedule, Dirk."

"It sure does," responded Dirk half grinning.

David walked over to Dirk and gave him a bear hug and a gripping handshake. "Our patients are really going to miss you. I'll be praying that everything goes well between you and your grandfather."

"Thank you, David."

Katherine took her turn to express her prayers as well. "Take care," she spoke meekly before giving him a final embrace.

The girls were sure to give Dirk one last hug. David and his family dismissed themselves, leaving Dirk and Elizabeth to have a few final moments to themselves.

Sitting hand in hand in silence, Dirk and Elizabeth heard the train outside come to a stop. Neither one could think of the right words to say. Simultaneously, they both stood as the conductor called for the passengers to begin boarding.

Dirk looked at Elizabeth. "That's me." He picked up his traveling bag with one hand and led Elizabeth outside onto the platform with the other.

Elizabeth spoke up trying to be cheerful. "Remember to send a wire when you arrive."

"I will," assured Dirk with a wink. "I'll be sure to let you know when I'm returning." Not a second after he finished speaking, he took Elizabeth in his arms and held her fast.

And not until the conductor made the final call for boarding did he release her. Dirk bent down and brushed her forehead with a kiss. He whispered words of love in her ear before reaching down, snatching up his bag, and ascending the steps to the train car.

He found a window seat on the side of the platform. He placed his bag overhead. As the train began to surge forward, he sat down and looked out. Beth stood waving with a smile on her face. Little did he know that tears were streaming down her cheeks. As the train moved on, she followed until she had gone the length of the platform. Elizabeth called out to him. Even though Dirk couldn't hear what she said, he knew in his heart that she had just expressed her love.

In a few short moments, she was no longer visible. He would always see her with his heart. The distance between them would grow vast, but the love they possessed for one another would keep them only a heartbeat away.

Printed in the United States
39567LVS00002B/85-132